You're a Real Hero, Amanda

You're a Real Hero, ❧ Amanda ❧

Arvella Whitmore

1985
Houghton Mifflin Company
Boston

Library of Congress Cataloging in Publication Data

Whitmore, Arvella.
  You're a real hero, Amanda.

  Summary: Devoted to her pet rooster, fifth-grader
Amanda determines to fight the law forbidding chickens
in town and runs into a series of unexpected problems.
  [1. City and town life—Fiction. 2. Pets—Fiction]
I. Title.
PZ7.W598Yo 1985   [Fic]   85-11738
ISBN 0-395-38950-X

Printed in the United States of America

V 10 9 8 7 6 5 4 3 2 1

To My Family,
and the
Minneapolis Branch AAUW Writers' Workshop

You're a Real Hero, Amanda

❦ *Chapter 1* ❦

Amanda glanced at the wall calendar and wrote September 21, 1931, in the upper right-hand corner of her paper. Miss Forbes took off ten points if you forgot the date.

"Quiet, class!" Miss Forbes rapped on her desk. She peered at Amanda through thick glasses that made her eyes seem twice their normal size. "Amanda Albee, what pet did you write about?"

Amanda stood. "My rooster." She wished her paper would stop shaking as she held it up. She cleared her throat and started to read. "Last summer my grandma said she wasn't feeling well. So she gave my mama her chickens because she couldn't take care of them. And she gave me one. A baby chick. It was tiny and yellow and real soft. She said it was all mine. So I took it home. I saw Grandma two days later. It was afternoon, and she was lying in bed. She took my hand and asked me how that little chick was and said I should take good care of it. I promised I would. Grandma died the next night. So I had this little chick and fed it every day. I gave it water, too, and held it and talked to it so it wouldn't get lonesome. It got bigger and bigger and changed so much you wouldn't believe it. It's grown up now and looks a lot different from the other chickens, because he turned out to be a rooster. And he's just beautiful. His feathers are brown, orange, and yellow. His tail is long and curvy and shines greenish-black in the sunlight. He likes it when I hold him. And he eats out of my hand."

Davy Butler, who sat two rows ahead of Amanda, raised his hand and waved it wildly.

Miss Forbes smiled and nodded. "Do you have something to say, Davy?" Davy Butler's daddy was the mayor of Prairie Bend. Miss Forbes liked Davy, but Amanda didn't. He was such a know-it-all.

Davy turned around and tilted his head in that cocky way Amanda hated so. "My daddy says there's a new law. And nobody in Prairie Bend will be allowed to keep chickens anymore."

Amanda gulped to choke down her anger. Davy always stomped on everything she said or did. But what if he was right? After all, his daddy was the mayor. Maybe there was a new law. Amanda's throat went dry and her knees started to shake. It was hard for her to pay attention as the others read their papers. All she could think about was her rooster and the new law.

When the three-thirty bell rang, Amanda darted out of the school building. Pushing against a strong, hot wind, she ran. She flew past the Latimers' Irish setter without stopping to pet him.

"I'll see you later, Clancy!" she yelled.

Her thoughts raced along with her feet. She didn't tell Miss Forbes everything about her rooster; like how she found his name, Mazda, printed on the end of a light bulb. She didn't want the whole fifth grade class laughing at her. She once made the mistake of telling her family her doll's name — Listerine. They laughed about that for days, though Amanda didn't think it was one bit funny.

A new law! So that was why Mama'd been killing more chickens than usual.

Panting hard, Amanda dashed to the chicken pen and looked through the big holes in the wire fence. They were still there! A dozen or more hens — some brown, some white — clucked and pecked the ground the same as ever. And in the middle stood Mazda, his green tail feathers rising above the flock. Amanda slipped around the gate and tiptoed up to Mazda. She lifted him and tucked him under her arm.

"I'm sorry, Mazda, but we'll have to hide you." Amanda stroked his feathers. Mama once said she wasn't to take him out of the pen. But Davy didn't say when the chickens had to go; if it was tonight, she'd be ready. Maybe men with nets would come in a truck like dogcatchers in big cities. She'd read about cities — and dogcatchers. Amanda looked around the yard. The space under the porch was no good. Too open. Next to the porch was a basement window. The coal room! Perfect. Nobody'd see him in there. Amanda knelt on the prickly grass, pried the window open, and set Mazda down on a heap of shiny coal.

"Now, you be good, Mazda, and stay real quiet."

"BWAWK!" replied Mazda.

"Shhh!" Amanda closed the window.

When she walked into the kitchen, Amanda smelled

roast chicken. Mama pushed wisps of brown hair back from her damp brow. "Amanda! Thank goodness you hurried home. I need your help." She peered into the cookstove oven. "I hope everything gets done in time."

"Are we having company?" Amanda reached into the cookie jar.

"Yes," said Mama, "the Harpools are coming to supper at six."

"Mama." Amanda bit into a graham cracker. "Have you heard about the new chicken law?"

"Why yes, Amanda," said Mama. "I don't know exactly when we'll have to get rid of our chickens. Not for several weeks, I'm sure."

Several weeks! Amanda was madder than ever at Davy Butler. She had lots of time to decide what to do about Mazda. She'd go down to the basement this minute, catch him, climb out the window with him, and put him back in the pen. She ran through the dining room to the basement door.

Margaret, who was setting the table, stepped in front of her. "Don't you dare hide down there, Amanda. You stay up here and help."

"I wasn't going to hide!" cried Amanda. Just because her sister was a year and a half older than Amanda didn't give her the right to be so bossy. Margaret and Amanda stood there glaring at each other. Daddy called Margaret "Princess," and she looked the part with her golden hair and dimples. Daddy had a pet name for Amanda, too, "Little Kitten," but Amanda would much rather be called "Princess." It wasn't fair, she thought, being the youngest and skinny, with freckles and stringy brown hair. Amanda stuck her tongue out at Margaret and went back into the kitchen. She'd sneak down to the basement as soon as she possibly could.

Amanda noticed a tall cake sitting by the sink. "Mama! I didn't know we were having angel food!"

"Mr. Schwartz brought eggs to help pay for his operation," said Mama, "so I made angel cake."

Amanda wished people paid doctors money instead of food, so they could afford one of those new gas stoves and an electric refrigerator.

"Is that the Mr. Schwartz Grandpa always talks about?" asked Amanda.

Mama lifted the mold off the Jell-O salad. "That's the one."

"Darn. I wanted to meet him." Amanda picked at the brown bits of cake left in the pan. Grandpa hated Mr. Schwartz. Amanda thought Grandpa's stories about him were exciting.

Margaret looked into the kitchen. Dimples flashed in her cheeks as she spoke. "What'll we do about the dishes, Mama? They don't match."

"Put the white plates between the flowered ones like a design." Mama straightened up and looked at both girls, but her glance lingered a bit longer on Amanda. "While the Harpools are here, I want you both to be on especially good behavior."

Amanda could tell Mama was nervous and she knew why. Mrs. Harpool was Prairie Bend's worst gossip. Grandpa called Mrs. Harpool "The Wireless" — not to her face, of course. Grandpa explained that when the radio was first invented, it was called the wireless, and that Mrs. Harpool was the best broadcasting machine he ever heard.

While Mama turned to count the places at the table, Amanda slipped out the back door. She'd catch Mazda from the coal room window. Suddenly she stopped and stared. A ragged man was coming up the walk. A tramp! Almost every week tramps stopped at the house for food, and Mama always fed them. Mama said most of them were probably nice men who rode freight trains and were just looking for work, but you could never be sure.

At the back steps, the tramp put down his knapsack and wiped his brow. "How about a sandwich for a hungry traveler, kid?"

"Wait here. I'll ask Mama." Amanda didn't like being called "kid."

Inside, Mama was mixing up icing for the cake. "Amanda, I don't have time. Make him some sandwiches, will you, dear?"

The tramp was sitting on the steps when Amanda handed him two peanut butter sandwiches on a plate and a glass of milk. She wondered if he was one of the nice ones, or the other kind.

"Are you a thief?" she asked.

The man looked up and laughed. Amanda could see that he was young and handsome under the layers of dirt.

"If I was, I'd be livin' a lot better," he said.

"Where'd you come from?" she asked.

"Chicago."

"Whew! I'd like to see a big city sometime." Amanda glanced at the basement window. "Want to see something beautiful? I'll show him to you."

"Sure. Why not?"

Amanda opened the basement window and squinted into the coal room blackness. Mazda was gone! He couldn't have gotten out! She stuck her head in and called to him. No sound. She reached in. No feathers. He had to be somewhere in the basement. She'd have to go down from inside as soon as she could.

Amanda turned to the tramp. "I can't find him right now, but I have the most beautiful rooster. His tail feathers are tall and shiny. And he has three tiny white dots on his comb. You have to look hard to see them. That makes him different from any other rooster in the whole world. His name is Mazda." Amanda giggled. "I'm not supposed to take him out of the pen." She looked into the window again. "He's down there somewhere. He has to be."

"If I had a fancy rooster," said the young man, "I'd train him to be a fighting cock. Then I'd take him down to Mexico and make a lot o' money."

Amanda closed the window. "What's a fighting cock?"

The tramp swallowed a cheekful of sandwich. "You put two roosters in a ring and they fight. And the one that wins makes his owner a pile o' money."

"What about the one that loses?"

The young man grinned at her with a crooked smile. "Gets killed."

7

Amanda gasped. "I think that's terrible. Where does the money come from?"

"Bets." His green eyes sparkled, and he winked at her.

Amanda didn't hear him at first. She was thinking about how cute he was. That wink! Those eyes! That lopsided grin! She liked him. Then all of a sudden she heard what he'd said and drew in a sharp breath. "That's gambling! That's as bad as whiskey!"

The tramp shook with silent laughter. "People out here in the sticks sure shock easily. If all you ever saw was this town, you'd never know these were modern times."

As Amanda stared at him, she heard someone call from the sidewalk.

"Hi, Amanda."

Amanda looked up and saw that it was Virginia Thornhill walking down the street. She carried a pink meat package tied with white string. Amanda thought Virginia was the prettiest high school girl in town, and there was something she'd been meaning to ask her. Amanda ran over to the fence.

"Hey, Virginia! I want to ask you something."

"Sure." As Virginia smiled, her eyes crinkled at the corners. Her hair was all different shades of shiny blond like the inlaid gold in Mama's locket.

"Do you eat oatmeal?" asked Amanda.

"Never touch it," said Virginia. "Why?"

"Mama says it'll make me pretty."

"My mother tells me the same thing, but I feed it to my dog." Virginia waved and walked on.

"Who's the good-lookin' dame?" asked the tramp.

"She's not a 'dame.' Her name is Virginia Thornhill, and her father owns the hardware store."

He smiled at Amanda, showing a row of even, white teeth. "Thanks."

What was he thanking her for? Amanda's knees felt weak. No doubt about it. She liked him.

"Amanda!" Mama was calling and holding the back door open.

After Amanda was inside, Mama said, "I want both you girls to stay right here until that tramp is gone. He may be all right, but you never know."

Amanda and Margaret sat by the window, licking the icing bowl, watching the tramp. At last he stood up. Amanda thought there was something wild and exciting about him. She noticed how straight his nose was in the matchlight as he lit a cigarette. He swung his knapsack over his shoulder with easy grace and wandered off. Goodbye, Tramp, she thought. They'd never see him again. In a way, it was probably a good thing. When she liked the shoe salesman at Zelinsky's, her big brother Hal and Margaret found out and teased her to tears. Hal said she had a "crush." He made it sound like a shameful disease — part infection and part joke.

All of a sudden, Amanda remembered Mazda. The basement! she thought. She had to go to the basement! If Mama found Mazda down there she'd be in real trouble. When she was sure that Mama and Margaret weren't watching, Amanda carefully stepped around the floor's squeaky spots, and was turning the door knob, when she heard Mama.

"Amanda! Please don't go down to the basement. You'll get dirty, and there's no time for a bath."

Amanda backed away. Mama and Miss Forbes had a lot in common — eyes and ears all around their heads.

Grandpa came in and hung up his hat. "Smells like we're eatin' high on the hog." He poked his head in the kitchen. "I hear we're goin' on the wireless tonight." He meant Mrs. Harpool. He tousled Amanda's hair. "How's my Indian Fighter today?"

Amanda grinned. Indian Fighter was Grandpa's pet name for her. He didn't have nicknames for Margaret or Hal. Daddy's father looked so much like a grandpa with his long white beard, white hair, and cane, that even Mama called him Grandpa.

Then Hal, Amanda's big brother, came in from selling *Saturday Evening Post* subscriptions. He wrinkled his freckled nose and said, "Mmmmmmm! When do we eat? I'm starved."

During the summer, Hal had grown so tall that his height still surprised Amanda whenever she saw him. His voice wavered and squawked sometimes and often sounded as low-pitched as Daddy's. He was too big now to play hide-and-seek; he stuck out of all the good hiding places.

Finally, Daddy opened the back door, set his black doctor case down, and put his arms around Mama. "How's my beautiful Martha tonight?" Then he kissed Mama before she could answer.

Amanda ran to Daddy and threw her arms around him. She loved the wool and tobacco and hospital smell of his coat. Daddy bent down so that the little bald spot showed in the center of his short, gray hair. He kissed Amanda on the cheek. "Hello, Little Kitten." Then he called to the others. "Hello, Princess! Hal! Father! Well, it looks like we're all here except the company."

"Oh, Howard, I'm so glad you aren't late," said Mama. "I want everything to be perfect."

Daddy hung up his coat. "Well, Martha, if I could just take the telephone off the hook, we'd be all set for the evening. Hey! Whose birthday is it? That's some cake!"

Mama smiled. "Mr. Schwartz brought eggs, and I subtracted fifteen cents from his bill. That's why the angel food. By the way, Howard, there's a call for you on the phone pad. I hope you won't have to go anywhere tonight."

Daddy picked up the telephone.

With the whole family around her, Amanda knew she'd have to wait to sneak down to the basement. But how long? Suppose Hal or Daddy went down there to put coal in the furnace? Not likely because the weather was warm. But Mama might go down to get a jar of pickles or something. She had to get Mazda out of there. Mama'd have a fit if she found out.

Grandpa pointed to the cake. "Martha, you don't need to give me any o' that."

"Why, Grandpa!" said Mama. "Don't you like angel food?"

"Angels had nothin' to do with it." Grandpa's bushy white eyebrows came together, and his eyes seemed deeper set than before. Amanda knew that look. It came over him whenever he thought about Mr. Schwartz.

"What do you mean?" asked Mama.

"I don't intend to eat anything that has Ol' Man Schwartz's eggs in it. You can tell that husband o' yours that he sold out to the enemy."

Amanda noticed Hal and Margaret watching Grandpa with round eyes. They liked hearing about Mr. Schwartz, too.

"But, Grandpa," said Mama, "he seemed polite when he brought the eggs. And he pays something on his bill every week."

"He stopped by the courthouse this afternoon where my old bunch was playin' dominoes," said Grandpa, "and tried to git some o' us fellas to make deliveries. He didn't say what for, but we suspect it's bootleggin'."

Amanda knew what bootleggers were. They were people who sneaked around and sold whiskey. She'd like to see a bootlegger sometime.

Mama gasped. "Why, Grandpa! That's illegal!"

"Well, that don't bother Ol' Man Schwartz," said Grandpa. "When none of us fellas showed any interest, he called us lazy bums. And that's not all he called us. Most of it, I can't repeat in front of you and the young folk."

Amanda wondered what bad words would do to her. She wanted to hear some.

"Shouldn't we tell the sheriff?" asked Mama.

"I talked to Sheriff Spear this afternoon," said Grandpa. "He said he doesn't have enough proof to arrest him. Same with that killin' a few years back. Everybody knew Schwartz did it, but nobody could nail him."

Daddy hung up the phone. "What's this all about?"

"Lester Schwartz," said Mama.

"I removed Lester's gallbladder two years ago." Daddy sighed. "Worst case of stones I ever saw." Daddy remembered people by their insides.

"Well, you didn't do a very good job," said Grandpa, " 'cause he's still got lotsa gall and plenty o' stones. You shoulda seen the rocks he was throwing around this afternoon."

Mama smiled at Daddy and said, "I hope the call wasn't urgent."

"No. Just a prescription."

"Good." Mama glanced at the wall clock and smoothed her hair into the bun at the back of her neck. She looked out the window and untied her apron. "Wash up, everyone. They're here!"

Oh no, thought Amanda. What about Mazda? No telling when she'd be able to rescue him.

❧ *Chapter 2* ❧

*W*hile she ate, Amanda kept an eye on the basement
door. There was no possible way she could leave the
table to go down there. So she amused herself by watching the fold of loose skin that hung down under Mrs.
Harpool's chin. It wiggled as she talked. Mama and
Daddy called Mrs. Harpool "Tess." Her husband's
name was Wilbur.

Mr. Harpool smiled. "It was so good of you to invite
us."

"Our pleasure, Wilbur. Our pleasure!" said Daddy.
Just then, the telephone rang.

"Oh, Howard," said Mama, "I was hoping that
wouldn't happen."

Daddy got up. "I'll get it. You all go right ahead and
eat."

The talk suddenly died down, and Daddy's voice
seemed louder than usual.

"Don't worry, Mrs. Morris," said Daddy. "Just wash
out his bowel with two quarts of warm soda water.
That's right, Mrs. Morris — two teaspoons of baking
soda to two quarts of water. I'll send out some pink,
chalky medicine. Give him a teaspoon of that every

four hours until the vomiting stops and his stool turns black. If he's not better by tomorrow afternoon, bring him in to the office."

Amanda's face grew hot. Didn't Daddy know they had company? Why couldn't he whisper? The telephone ought to be moved to the back bedroom. Of course, the Albee family went right on eating, since they were used to hearing that prescription. Amanda noticed, though, that Mr. and Mrs. Harpool looked at each other and pushed the food around on their plates with their forks.

Then Mrs. Harpool started talking to Mama as though her mouth was driven by a high-speed motor. Amanda could see why Grandpa called her The Wireless.

"That Morris boy being sick doesn't surprise me one bit," said Mrs. Harpool. "The way Alva Morris allows her children to run around eating sweets at all hours is a disgrace. Those children never get the nourishment they need. I know for a fact the Morrises never serve oatmeal at their house."

Oatmeal! Amanda was sick to death of hearing about oatmeal, the miracle food. Ugh! Hal winked at her from across the table.

Amanda could tell from Mama's strained smile that she felt uneasy hearing all that gossip about the Morrises. She didn't say a word. But when Mrs. Harpool mentioned oatmeal, Mama latched onto her favorite subject. "Tess," she said, "I agree with you about oatmeal. It's a fine food. If you want healthy, beautiful children, feed them plenty of good hot oatmeal."

Amanda took a deep breath and said, "Virginia Thornhill never eats oatmeal, and she's the prettiest girl in town. I asked her. She told me."

Grandpa hid his mouth behind his napkin. Amanda knew he was laughing.

Mrs. Harpool turned to Amanda. Her eyes narrowed as she seemed to rewind her gears for another round of gossip. "Stick to your oatmeal, young lady. You wouldn't want to turn out like that Virginia Thornhill."

"Why not?" asked Amanda. The thought that she could possibly turn out like Virginia Thornhill someday gave Amanda the greatest pleasure.

"If you ask me," said Mrs. Harpool, "Walter Thornhill spoils that Virginia rotten. He said he taught her to drive his car so she could run errands for him. I'll tell you right now, he doesn't get many errands out of that girl! You should see the way she streaks around in that automobile with five or six of her friends — some of them boys. And she spends a fortune on silk stockings, wearing them to school every day the way she does. And now she's taken to putting on lipstick. I tell you, when a young woman flaunts herself, trouble's not far away."

"What does *flaunt* mean, Mrs. Harpool?" asked Amanda.

"You'll find out when you're older," said Mrs. Harpool.

Amanda hated it when people said she had to be older to learn certain words.

Mrs. Harpool took a sip of water. Refueled, she continued, "Now Virginia's older sister Dorothy is a different story entirely. Have you heard her play that violin? Dorothy just sticks to her music, and as far as I know, never has time for the boys."

"I play the violin, too," said Margaret. "And if I practice real hard, I may get to be in the Christmas recital." For two years, Margaret had taken lessons from Mr. Gilly across the street. Amanda thought her practicing sounded awful. And depend on Margaret to chime in just then when Mrs. Harpool was praising Dorothy. The meaning of it was perfectly clear to Amanda. Margaret played the violin and ate her oatmeal like a good girl. And, like a bad girl, Amanda had crushes and fed her oatmeal to Mazda. It added up like simple arithmetic; Margaret was like Dorothy, and Amanda like Virginia. But in spite of everything Mrs. Harpool said, Amanda felt pleased about it.

When Daddy came back to the table, Mrs. Harpool said, "Doctor, we were just discussing Walter Thornhill's daughter Dorothy. She'll be playing the violin on the radio one of these days!"

Grandpa looked Mrs. Harpool in the eye and laughed under his breath. "Amazing machine, the wireless. It picks up the tiniest sound, and before you know it, it goes all over the world."

Amanda held her breath. Would Mrs. Harpool guess Grandpa was talking about her?

Mrs. Harpool stared at Grandpa for about two seconds, speechless for once. Then, with a frown, she turned to Mama. "Has Mr. Albee been feeling all right lately?"

Mama raised her eyebrows. "Oh, fine, Tess. Just fine."

Mrs. Harpool lowered her voice. "Well, when people get to be his age, you never know."

Somebody ought to change the subject, thought Amanda. She glanced at the basement door and said the first thing that popped into her head. "Mrs. Harpool, do you like roosters?"

"Roosters?" Mrs. Harpool stared at Amanda, then she turned to Mama. "Have you heard about Mayor Butler's new chicken law, Martha? I'll never vote for that man again! What he won't think of next!"

Amanda couldn't wait to hear more about the chicken law. "How long can we keep our chickens, Mrs. Harpool?"

"Well now, I heard Mayor Butler himself say that all our chickens must be gone by the end of November."

The end of November! Amanda felt like shouting for joy. More than two whole months! She had all the time in the world to make plans for Mazda!

"We'll certainly miss the fresh eggs and meat," said Mama.

"Mayor Butler is trying to make conditions in Prairie Bend more sanitary," said Daddy.

"That chicken law is a bunch o' highfalutin' nonsense," said Grandpa. "I'm goin' to do all I can to work against it."

Grandpa was right. Amanda stared at the basement door. The new law had to be stopped. She'd work against it, too.

"It's a free country," said Grandpa. "If you don't like a law, it's up to you to try and change it."

Change it! Amanda wanted to get up that minute and do a cartwheel, she felt so excited. That's what she'd do with that crazy old chicken law! She'd change it! She had two months! She was saving bits of food on her napkin for Mazda. After dinner, she'd sneak down to the basement, catch Mazda, feed him, climb out the coal room window, and put him in the pen.

After dessert, Mama stood up. "Why don't we have our second cup of coffee in the living room? You children put away the food and stack the dishes."

Amanda tiptoed to the basement door.

"Oh, no you don't," said Margaret. "You stay up here and help."

"I'll be right back. Honest!"

But when Amanda opened the door she couldn't believe her eyes. With a feathery swoosh, Mazda sailed into the dining room as if he'd been shot upstairs by a hidden spring. Broken glass tinkled as he landed on the dining room table. Amanda stood there with her hands cupped over her mouth, while Mazda screeched an excited "BWAWK! BWAWK! BWAWK!"

Mrs. Harpool screamed and ran to the other side of the room.

Mama shouted, "My stars! How did that chicken get in here?"

Everyone gasped as Mazda soared through the air and perched on Mr. Harpool's shiny bald head. For some crazy reason, Amanda stood there thinking how

Mazda's colorful plumes looked like tribal headdresses she had seen in *National Geographic*. Mr. Harpool's jaw dropped as he ducked and brushed the rooster away. His cup and saucer clattered to the floor; coffee soaked into one of the rug's pink roses, staining it brown.

Mama and Daddy'll kill him! thought Amanda. They'll kill him!

Then Mazda flew up to a closed window, snarling himself in the lace curtain. The harder he struggled, the more tangled he became.

"BUCK, BUCK, BUH KAWP!" he shrieked.

"My curtains!" Mama threw up her hands.

"Merciful heavens!" shouted Mrs. Harpool. "I may faint!"

With shaking fingers, Amanda grabbed Mazda and held him while Daddy freed his claws from the shredded lace. Then, with a screech, he flapped away, and lit on the silk lamp shade, toppling the stand with a crash.

Mrs. Harpool yelled, "I've never seen anything like this in my whole life! With all this excitement, I could have a heart attack. I'm so glad you're right here in this room, Doctor."

Mama dived for the rooster's legs and missed.

Mazda flew against one wall and then another, leaving black coal dust on everything he touched. A candlestick fell and rolled across the floor as he cleared a spot for himself on the polished sideboard. Everyone circled around him.

"I can catch him right now!" cried Amanda.

"You've done enough catching already, young lady," said Mama.

It was a bad sign when Mama called Amanda "young lady." She shuddered.

After Mama caught Amanda's rooster and put him back in the pen, the Harpools left. Mrs. Harpool said she'd have to "take to her bed" immediately to calm her racing heart. Then Amanda cleaned up Mazda's mess as Mama pointed out one dirty or broken thing after another. Finally, Mama and Daddy sat side by side in the kitchen, and ordered Amanda to stand in front of them. Grandpa, Hal, and Margaret had all gone to their rooms.

"Well, young lady," said Daddy, "What do you have to say for yourself?"

Young lady again. It was bad. Amanda bit her lower lip. "You're not going to kill him, are you, Mama?"

Mama squeezed her lips into a thin line, and her eyes glared ice-blue. "We'll see."

Amanda knew that "We'll see" was no answer at all. She shook with sobs. "I didn't think he could get out of the coal bin."

Daddy stood up. "The sooner we get this over with, the better we'll all feel."

"Oh no!" cried Amanda.

Daddy led her to the back porch, sat on a feed sack, and placed Amanda across his knee. The spanking stung. Amanda counted the whacks. Six in all.

*

Later, as she lay awake beside the sleeping Margaret, Amanda felt someone stroke her hair. Then she heard Mama's voice.

"We don't approve of what you did, but we understand why you did it, Amanda."

"Are you going to kill him, Mama?"

"No, dear. You can keep your rooster until Thanksgiving. We'll give him away then, but he must be left in the pen. Is that clear?"

"Yes, Mama."

Amanda wondered why everything she did caused trouble. Take Margaret. She was absolutely perfect, and never did anything wrong. Hal did wrong things sometimes, but he was pretty sneaky about them and seldom got caught.

When the house had grown dark and quiet, Amanda got up and tiptoed to the kitchen. A moonbeam shimmered across the oilcloth table cover, turning its red tulips black. She stood on a chair and took the flashlight from the shelf above the cookstove. Back in the bedroom, Amanda picked up her school tablet. The tearing of paper ripped through the silence, and bedsprings twanged as Margaret turned over on her side. Amanda froze and listened, but her sister slept on. Amanda found a pencil and crawled under the bed. The blankets hanging down made a perfect secret tent.

Lying in a dim circle of light, Amanda started to write. Tomorrow she'd slip the letter into the newspaper's mailbox. The chicken law had to be changed. She wasn't about to give up Mazda.

She wrote on, but something kept humming like a tune in the back of her mind. Over and over she heard it. She tried not to listen, but she couldn't shut it out. It said, "Nobody listens to a kid."

❦ Chapter 3 ❦

*A*manda checked the front porch, but the morning paper hadn't come yet. Her letter hadn't been in yesterday's paper. Maybe today's. She ran around back to gather the eggs. When she saw Mazda, she set her basket down and picked him up. She held him in her arms and stroked his feathers.

"Don't you worry, Mazda. I'll take care of you. We're not going to let anybody take you away. And nobody's mad at you about the other night. It was all my fault."

When Amanda went in with the eggs, Mama was placing the ice card in the window. The four numbers on it, facing in different directions, 25, 50, 75, and 100, stood for pounds. Whichever number the ice man saw right side up, was the weight of the block he'd bring in.

Amanda heard voices in the dining room. When she looked in, she saw that the back cover was off their radio, and Hal and Daddy were inspecting its insides.

Amanda skipped over to them. "Let me help."

"Beat it," said Hal. "This is a grown-up job." Amanda just stood there. She was tired of being treated like dirt because she was the youngest. And after the Harpool dinner it had gotten worse.

Hal spoke to Daddy in his lowest tones. "The batteries seem all right. I'll bet if we replaced that dead tube, it'd work just fine."

"I'm more than happy to turn this case over to you, son," said Daddy. "Not enough blood and guts in it for me!" Daddy always talked about people's insides. Amanda wondered what it would be like to have a normal man for a father.

From the kitchen, Mama cried, "Howard! Such language!"

"What's wrong with blood and guts? We all have 'em, and I fix 'em." Daddy kissed Mama. "What's for breakfast, Martha?"

"Buckwheat cakes, and they're on the table."

"Mmmmmm!" said Daddy. "My favorite food cooked by my favorite girl. Who needs heaven?"

Dimples dotted Mama's cheeks as she laughed. "I think you had too much sleep last night, Howard. You're not used to it."

Daddy, Mama, Hal, Margaret, and Amanda sat down at the kitchen table. Grandpa wasn't up yet. Daddy no sooner sat down, than he got up to answer a knock at the back door. There stood Mr. Cox, the ice man, holding a fifty-pound frozen block on his back with huge iron tongs. The ice dripped on the porch floor.

"Why, good morning, Ed," said Daddy. "I was just thinking about you the other day. How's that aching back?"

"Well, it's better, Doc, but it still pains me once in a while." It wasn't hard for Amanda to see why he had a backache. She wondered why Daddy didn't tell him

25

to quit all that lifting. Mama opened the icebox door, and Mr. Cox slid his heavy load into it.

"Is fifty pounds all you want? I hear it's gonna be hot for a couple o' days."

"Fifty'll be fine," said Mama.

Daddy pulled out a chair. "Here, Ed, sit down and have some buckwheat cakes."

Mr. Cox grinned. "Don't mind if I do!" He took the thick leather shield off his back. "I'll put this out on the porch so it don't get your floor all wet." Amanda liked Mr. Cox. He always let kids climb into his truck and take pieces of ice to lick.

"How's business these days, Ed?" asked Daddy.

"Terrible," said Mr. Cox. "With fall comin' on now, and with them new 'lectric machines that freeze ice cubes in little trays, my business has sure fallen off."

Amanda wished they'd get one of those new Frigidaires, so she could freeze her own lemonade suckers.

Mr. Cox poured syrup on his pancakes. "I tell ya, Doc, the pictures of them soup lines in the paper scare ya to death. If I lose any more customers, I'll be right there with 'em. And that new law sayin' we have to get rid of our cow is sure goin' to hurt." Mr. Cox took a bite of pancake. "I suppose you folks'll be gettin' rid o' your chickens before long."

Amanda stiffened. The chicken law! She wondered if the paper was here yet. If she'd known about the cow part, she would have mentioned it in her letter. Maybe she'd write another one.

Mama sighed. "We'll soon have to decide what to do with the chickens we don't eat." Mama talked as if the chicken law was a sure thing. Why wasn't she fighting it? She didn't seem to care.

Mr. Cox finished his pancakes and stood up. "That tasted mighty good. I musta been hungrier than I thought. I sure do thank you folks."

Amanda had an idea. She whispered in Mama's ear.

Mama smiled. "Why, yes, Amanda. Go ahead."

Amanda lifted yesterday's newspaper from the stack by the sink, the one with the soup line pictures, crumpled it, stuffed it into an old coffee can, then carefully set several eggs inside. She held it out to Mr. Cox and said, "Here. For you. I gathered them this morning."

"Why, thank you, Amanda. I'll find a way to pay you back, young lady. You just see if I don't. I have to run along now."

Daddy shook hands with Mr. Cox. "It was good to see you, Ed."

After Mr. Cox left, Grandpa rushed into the kitchen holding up the morning paper. "Guess which one of the Albees made the news this morning!"

Excitement shook Amanda's whole body, but she said nothing. She couldn't guess how Mama and Daddy would feel about her letter. After what happened the other night, Mazda wasn't exactly their favorite chicken. And though she didn't want to think about it, with all the trouble she caused, she couldn't be their favorite child either.

"Well?" said Grandpa.

Daddy said, "I haven't the faintest idea, Father. Who?"

"Come on, now. Guess!" Grandpa's eyes sparkled with joy.

Mama said, "It must be about you, Howard, at that medical meeting in Kansas City."

"Nope." Grandpa shook his head. "Guess again."

"I've got it," said Daddy. "Martha's book review at Ladies' Aid."

"Nope."

A slow grin spread across Mama's face. "Hal won an award as best *Post* salesman."

"Guess again."

Daddy smiled. "Margaret made the honor roll."

" 'Tain't about Margaret."

They'd stop guessing long before her name came up, thought Amanda.

"Then it has to be about you, Grandpa!" said Hal.

"Nope. You get one more guess."

Then Mama laughed. "Don't tell me it's Amanda!"

Always last! thought Amanda. And those words! "Don't tell me it's AMANDA!" And Mama had laughed! Amanda's stomach knotted into a fist.

"Well, you finally got it right." Grandpa put the paper down in front of Mama and pointed. "There 'tis. Amanda here wrote a dandy letter to the paper. It's short and snappy and right to the point. I couldn't o' done better myself."

The whole family gasped, "AMANDA?" and stared at her in disbelief.

"Read it to us, Martha," said Daddy.

Mama cleared her throat and read, " 'I think Mayor Butler's chicken law is bad. People need their chickens for eggs and meat. Besides, I want to keep my pet rooster. Signed, Amanda Albee.' "

"Ain't that a dandy?" Grandpa beamed.

Mama and Daddy smiled at each other and didn't say much. They never said much when she did something. They said plenty whenever Hal or Margaret did anything. But she was the youngest, and the youngest didn't count. At least that's the way it seemed.

Grandpa patted Amanda on the shoulder. "I'm mighty proud of my Indian Fighter right now. Together we'll win this battle."

Amanda smiled up at him and squeezed his hand. At least Grandpa took her seriously.

Before she left for school, Amanda went into the chicken pen, picked Mazda up, and fed him some of her breakfast pancake.

"Mazda," she said, "they printed our letter in the paper. And hundreds and hundreds of people will read it and make Mayor Butler change his mind about that silly old chicken law. Then you'll be able to stay here forever as my pet. Isn't that wonderful, Mazda?"

"BUCK KAWP!" he replied.

The first bell hadn't rung yet, when Davy Butler stopped Amanda on the playground. "Hey, Amanda! You know what my Dad did when he read your letter?"

Amanda tried to keep the excitement out of her voice. "No. What did he do?"

"He laughed his head off."

A lump rose in Amanda's throat, and her stomach felt queasy. "Didn't he say anything?"

"Sure. He said Amanda Albee takes after her goofy grandpa."

"My grandpa's not goofy!" she yelled. Her face burned with anger.

"That's not all!" cried Davy. "I hear you have chickens running all over your house."

Mrs. Harpool's work, thought Amanda. Every nerve in her body wanted to hit Davy, throw him on the ground, and kick the daylights out of him, but he was bigger than she was. When she tried to stare him down, she blinked, and hot tears stung her cheeks. She turned and ran to the school building. The nerve! How could someone as mean as Davy's father become mayor of a town? And Davy was nasty. He should talk about chickens! The other day he told the class he had a pet salamander. Ugh! At the door, she turned around and saw Davy watching her. She stuck out her tongue.

❦ *Chapter 4* ❦

Since Amanda was late, she felt lucky that Mama was away at Ladies' Aid. She had to stay after school because Miss Forbes caught her making faces at Davy Butler. Hattie, who was ironing in the kitchen, didn't watch the clock the way Mama did.

"Hello, Hattie." Amanda went straight to the phone book in the dining room and ran her finger down the B's. She found him. Butler, Frank P., Office of the Mayor, Courthouse. The courthouse! Everybody knew where that was! The phone number was right there too. 684. Should she call him? She glanced into the kitchen. Hattie would hear her and might tell Mama. She'd wait.

Hattie glided the iron over Amanda's blue dotted dress, changing it from limp and puckered to satiny smooth. Ironing was not all Hattie did. She often helped Daddy deliver babies in poor people's homes when the mother couldn't afford to go to the hospital. For months, Amanda had been trying to work up the nerve to ask Hattie about babies being born. The only thing she knew for sure was that a woman got fat before she had a baby. What better time, she thought, than right now, while they were alone? She'd work up to the subject slowly. That way, Hattie wouldn't be so apt to clam up.

"You iron pretty," said Amanda. "I like to watch you." She wasn't sure where to go on from there.

"Well, I try," Hattie held up her chocolate-brown hand and wiggled her fingers. " 'Course the magic in these helps, too. By the way, your Mama wants you to go to Thornhill's to buy a radio tube exactly like that one lyin' there on the table."

"Aw, do I have to?" Amanda's nerve was shot to pieces by this sudden order.

"That's what your mama says, and what your mama says is law aroun' here."

"Shucks!" Just like Mama. Sending her to the store because everybody else was too busy doing more important things. Hal with his magazine route, and Margaret with her violin lessons. Sure. Send Amanda. She's just a little kid and doesn't have anything more important to do.

As soon as Amanda was out the door, she made a decision. Since she was going downtown anyway, and now that she knew where the mayor's office was, she'd do an errand of her own. She put the radio tube in her sweater pocket and ran to the chicken pen. She cornered Mazda, picked him up, and cradled him in her arms.

"BUCK KAWP!" said Mazda.

"It's all right, Mazda," said Amanda. "Mama's not here, and I'll put you back before she comes home. After we go to Thornhill's, I'm taking you over to Mayor Butler's office. When he sees how pretty you are, he's sure to change his mind about that silly chicken law."

At the hardware store, Mr. Thornhill peered down at Amanda through his spectacles and took the radio tube. He kept glancing at Mazda. Amanda hoped she wouldn't have to put him outdoors.

"So that's your pet rooster," he said.

Amanda held Mazda up by his yellow legs so Mr. Thornhill could get a better look.

"That's some bird all right. Handsome tail feathers." He grinned. "I saw your letter in the paper this morning. Know something? I agree with you one hundred percent."

Amanda liked Mr. Thornhill. He talked and joked with her when she came into the store. As she tucked Mazda under her arm, a wave of anger flashed over her again at Davy Butler's mean words. She looked up at Mr. Thornhill and said, "I wish you were our mayor."

Mr. Thornhill laughed. "If I were, I'd make you my chief adviser." He turned the radio tube over in his hands. "Well, Amanda, I'm not sure I have a part exactly like this. I'll check and see, though." Then he called out, "Jack? Come here a minute."

Amanda caught her breath when a young man came out from the back room. It was the same one who had eaten her sandwiches on their back steps. A strange little thrill ran down her spine.

"Jack, I'm going to the stockroom. Mind the store, will you?"

After Mr. Thornhill left, Jack smiled at Amanda

with one side of his mouth. "I see you found my fighting cock."

Amanda just stood there and felt herself blush. Why couldn't he have left town?

Jack held out his hands. "Let me see him."

Amanda affected a snooty voice and held Mazda closer. "He's not your fighting cock. He's my pet. Wanting him doesn't make him yours."

"Scrappy little kid, aren't you?" said Jack. "Well, I guess it takes all kinds. This town sure seems to have 'em."

Amanda noticed that he was quite handsome now that he was all cleaned up. Must be about twenty, she thought. His green eyes lighted up his tan face. She blushed again. "Wh—— wh—— when did you start working here?" She stammered and her voice shook. Cut it out! she told herself. He'll surely notice.

"I just walked in here after I left your place, and the old man put me to work."

Amanda knew one way to hide her crush. Act like she hated him. In her fiercest voice, she said, "His name is Mr. Thornhill, and he's not an old man. He's middle-aged like my daddy."

"Okay! Okay! Don't get so hot under the collar!"

"And don't say okay. My mama says it's not a real word."

"Well, you tell your mama she can give me speakin' lessons when she brings me a piece o' that cake I saw through your window." Jack smiled his funny, crooked smile, and winked at her.

Amanda's face got fiery hot. He knew. How could he

help it? She was never any good at hiding her feelings. She turned her back on him and brushed her free hand across the rollers of a skate on display.

In a minute, Mr. Thornhill came back. "Here's a tube. It's not exactly like the one you brought in, but I think it'll work."

When Amanda left the store, a cool rain started to fall. It felt good on her burning face. To keep him from getting too wet, she slipped Mazda under her sweater. As she started across the street to the courthouse, she saw Mama come out of Zelinsky's Dry Goods. Ladies' Aid must be over! Amanda hid between two parked cars and watched. Her hands got cold, and her knees shook.

"She'll kill us both if she sees us," she whispered to Mazda. But instead of turning toward home, Mama went into Reuter's grocery. Good! If she hurried, Amanda figured she'd have enough time to visit the mayor's office. She ran across the street and, slinking behind a row of cars parked in front of the square, made her way to the courthouse.

The upper half of the heavy door had a frosted glass panel with black printing on it that said THE OFFICE OF THE MAYOR. Amanda turned the brass knob and went in. From a high wooden counter, a woman with glasses and a gray braid around the top of her head looked down at her. She didn't seem to notice Mazda.

"I'd like to see Mayor Butler," said Amanda.

"Do you have an appointment?"

"No. But I have something to show him." Amanda held Mazda up high so that the lady could see. Mazda

35

flapped his wings, fanning the papers on the counter so that they blew every which way.

"Mercy!" exclaimed the gray-haired lady as she gathered up the scattered sheets.

"I'm sorry," said Amanda. "I'll help." Amanda set Mazda down on a chair and helped the lady gather up her papers. With a screech, Mazda flew up and perched on the counter.

The lady screamed, "Get that rooster out of here!"

An inside door with a frosted glass panel marked PRIVATE flew open, and a heavy man with bushy gray hair rushed out. "What's going on here?" he demanded in a booming voice.

The lady pointed her finger at Amanda. "Mayor Butler, that child brought a rooster in here."

"So I see. So I see!"

Amanda held Mazda under her arm. So this was Davy's father. Could he have said all those nasty things?

"Well! Well!" said Mayor Butler. "You must be Amanda Albee! Good to meet ya young lady, good to meet ya." Mayor Butler held out his right hand. Amanda's right hand was holding Mazda, so she gave him her left.

"This is Mazda," said Amanda, "the pet rooster I wrote about."

"Well, well!" cried Mayor Butler. "Isn't he a beauty! A real beauty! What did you say his name was?"

"Mazda."

"Mazda." Mr. Butler seemed to listen to himself say it. "Mazda. A fine name! A fine name!" Then he turned to the lady. "Eleanor, hand me the candy box."

He flipped open a Whitman's Sampler and said, "Tell you what — I'm real glad you brought Magna in here to see me —"

"Mazda." Amanda corrected him.

"Mazda. As I was saying, I'm real glad you brought him in here to see me, but I have someone waiting in my office back there." Mayor Butler held out the box. "Have a chocolate."

After Amanda chose what she hoped would be a vanilla cream, Mr. Butler pushed her gently toward the outer door. "Real glad you came, Amanda. Real glad. Pretty bird you have there. Mighty pretty bird."

Before she knew it, Amanda found herself out in the hall, staring up at the closed door. Mayor Butler's shadow disappeared behind the frosted glass as the sticky caramel tangled in her teeth.

It was so quick, thought Amanda, as she and Mazda made their way home through the rain. She was out of his office before she had a chance to say anything about the new law. But he saw how pretty Mazda was. He said so himself. That was the important thing. When Amanda put Mazda back in the pen, she said, "I think Mayor Butler liked you."

"Buck, buck, buck, buck," said Mazda.

When she went into the house, Amanda was pleased that Hattie was still at the ironing board. Mama wasn't home yet. When Amanda found herself alone with Hattie, she decided to finish what she had started earlier — asking about babies. There couldn't be much time left, so she came right out with it.

"Hattie," she said, "how are babies born?"

"Oh, now honey, don't you devil me with a question like that! When your mama wants you to know about babies bein' born, she'll tell you herself. It ain't up to me to tell you 'bout such things."

"I heard you were there with Daddy when the Hinkle twins came. What'd you do?"

Hattie rolled her eyes. "Oh, Lordy! Why don't you ask your Daddy? He'd tell you."

"My mama won't let him."

"She must have some good reason, then."

"She has a book that explains it all," said Amanda. "She let Hal read it two years ago. Margaret's going to read it on her birthday in March. She made Hal promise not to tell us what's in it. Then Margaret'll promise not to tell me. I've looked for it, but I can't find it."

Hattie heaved a sigh. "Now don't you go lookin' for things your mama don't want you to find. That's no way to do."

Grown-ups! Trying to understand them was like looking through the frosted glass doors in Mayor Butler's office. You could see shadows moving around but you couldn't tell what they were doing. Daddy had a frosted glass door dividing his examining room from the waiting room. Amanda sometimes made a game of guessing what the gray shapes behind the glass really looked like. Then when the patients came out, they were often nothing like she'd imagined.

The starch water boiling on the cookstove fogged the kitchen windows. It gave the room a closed-in feeling. With her finger, Amanda drew a tiny outline of Mazda on the steamy glass, then rubbed the middle part clear.

When she looked through the peephole, she saw Mama coming up the walk.

"Hattie," asked Amanda, "why do grown-ups keep so many secrets from kids?"

"Honey, I reckon grown-ups don't keep any more secrets from kids than kids keeps from grown-ups."

Amanda drew in a deep breath. "You're smart, Hattie."

Mama came in the back door. "Hello, Hattie! Hello, Amanda! Why, Hattie! You put the stew pot on! Bless you. You think of everything!"

"Well, I knew you'd be needin' supper soon."

Mama handed Hattie a fifty cent piece. "Hattie, since you live outside town, I want you to take our chickens at Thanksgiving time — the ones we haven't eaten. Everyone at Ladies' Aid was talking about how Mayor Butler will start fining people the Friday after Thanksgiving."

Every muscle in Amanda's body froze. No wonder Mayor Butler rushed her out of his office! Davy was right! His dad had paid no attention to her letter. He probably had laughed just the way Davy said. And he probably had called Grandpa "goofy."

"I sure could use them chickens, Mrs. Albee," said Hattie.

"Oh, Hattie!" cried Amanda. "Don't take my rooster!"

Hattie dropped the fifty cent piece into her apron pocket. "Well, honey, you jes' make up your mind, now. Would you rather eat him or have me take him?"

Amanda looked from one to the other. Her stomach felt like it had fallen to her knees.

Mama hugged Amanda. "I told you we'd be giving him away, dear. And I know it will be hard for you. But the mayor and the city council voted on the chicken law last week. Your letter was too late."

Tears slipped down Amanda's cheeks. "But I promised Grandma —"

Margaret burst into the room and stopped. "What's the matter?"

"Amanda's upset about her rooster," said Mama.

Margaret put her violin case down. "Guess what! Mr. Gilly said I could be in the Christmas recital!"

"Congratulations, dear," said Mama.

Margaret the Perfect, thought Amanda. Did anyone really doubt she'd be in the recital? Margaret always got what she wanted. It was hard not to hate Margaret sometimes. You'd never catch Margaret doing anything as crazy as loving a rooster she couldn't keep. No. Amanda couldn't imagine Margaret loving a rooster at all.

Hal came in and threw his canvas *Saturday Evening Post* bag down on the kitchen table. "I just sold subscriptions to Mrs. Spriggs and Mrs. Latimer!"

"Good for you!" said Mama.

It wasn't fair, thought Amanda. Hal and Margaret's lives were two big success stories. Disgusting!

"Did you get the radio tube, Amanda?" asked Hal.

"It's on the dining room table." Amanda's voice was choked with tears, but Hal didn't seem to notice. He didn't even thank her for going downtown to get his darn old radio tube. Amanda dried her eyes and made up her mind to keep Mazda in spite of Hattie and Mama and Mayor Butler.

"Don't forget, Hattie," said Mama. "I'll need you next month on Ladies' Aid Day."

"I'll be here, Mrs. Albee. I'd rather hide away on that Pullman car with m' husband and see all them mountains out west. But I reckon I'll jes' have to wait 'til I git to heaven." Hattie's chest rose up, then down, in a deep sigh. "Yep. I'll be here."

"Do they have mountains in heaven, Hattie?" asked Amanda.

"Oh, you betcha, honey. They got everything in heaven. 'Bye now."

Amanda liked Hattie. She either answered your questions straight out or refused.

As Amanda helped Margaret and Mama set the table, she said, "Guess who I saw working at Thornhill's store today?"

Mama handed Amanda the napkins. "Who, dear?"

"That tramp who came to our back door the other day."

Mama paused a second. "Really?"

Margaret stopped and stared at Amanda. "Him? Are you sure?"

"It's the same one. He even said so, and his name is Jack." Amanda put a napkin at each place. "I don't like him." After she said that, Amanda realized that the lie wasn't really necessary.

From the front room came squeals and static and the voice of a news announcer.

The back door swung open and Daddy walked in.

"It's working!" Hal shouted. They all gathered around the radio and listened long enough to hear the voice say, "President Hoover told reporters today that recovery from the Depression is just around the corner."

Daddy put his arm around Hal and said, "Hal, you did a good job of breathing life into that old radio. Should be all right for several more years." Daddy patted Hal's back. "I'm real proud of you. Yes, Hal, your mother and I are both proud of you."

As Amanda put the knives and forks at the places, she tried to imagine how Hal must feel after such praise from Daddy. Then a funny thing happened. Amanda felt as though Hal's success had sucked away every drop of good feeling in her. She felt hollow and worthless, like an empty shell. She was just the little kid nobody paid any attention to, the good-for-nothing kid other people sent to the store. Then from somewhere, a flood of fighting spirit poured into her. Amanda gritted her teeth and said to herself, "I'll show 'em. The very next time the radio breaks down, I'll fix it all by myself."

Later, as Amanda fed Mazda leftover bits of beef stew, she crouched down and whispered. "Mazda, I don't know yet how we're going to do this, but you're going to stay with me. I may have to move you to some secret place, but you'll get used to it. Now, don't you worry. I won't let them take you away. I'll put you someplace where I can visit you every day and bring you part of my supper. I promise."

"BWAWK, BWAWK, BWAWK," replied Mazda.

❧ *Chapter 5* ❧

*T*hanksgiving tomorrow! Mazda's time was up! Amanda dropped her schoolbooks on the dining room table. Her breath came fast.

"Mama, when is Hattie coming to pick up the chickens?"

"At seven."

"Tonight?" Amanda swallowed. Panic itched at her scalp.

"Yes. Tonight." Mama looked up from the sewing machine. "Amanda, see who's at the back door, will you, dear?"

"But Mama!" cried Amanda. "I have to go to Louise's right now." Her best friend, Louise Spriggs, had promised to help her hide Mazda.

"Answer the door, please, dear."

"Then may I go?"

"We'll see," said Mama.

No "we'll see" about it, thought Amanda. She'd go. She'd sneak out her window if she had to.

When Amanda opened the door, a heavyset man dressed in a shiny black suit stood on the back porch. He was holding a large pumpkin.

"Where's your ma?" he asked.

"She's sewing in the other room," said Amanda. "Come on in. I'll call her."

The man said, "Ain't you takin' a chance, miss? As far as you know, I could be a tramp." He had bushy eyebrows, and long hairs hung from his nostrils. He glared at Amanda with small black eyes.

Amanda felt herself stretch to her full height. "Tramps don't carry pumpkins, and they don't wear suits."

When the man spoke, he showed jagged yellow teeth. Some were missing on the sides. "Proud little filly, ain't ya? I'll tell ya right now, I'd take the sass out o' ya in a hurry if you was mine."

What did that mean? Amanda wondered. Take the sass out of her? Just what would he do to her? She was glad she wasn't his and felt sorry for anyone who was.

Mama walked into the kitchen and said, "Why, Mr. Schwartz! What a nice-looking pumpkin. This is our daughter Amanda."

Amanda stood there frozen. So this was Mr. Schwartz! The man Grandpa hated so! She wanted to ask him if he was really a bootlegger and whether he'd ever killed anyone, but she couldn't in front of Mama.

"How are you, Mr. Schwartz?" asked Mama.

"Not too bad," he said. "My missus does enough complainin' fer both of us."

Amanda glanced at the clock. She'd leave in five minutes flat no matter what.

Mama cleared a place on the kitchen table for the pumpkin. "What's wrong with Mrs. Schwartz?"

"Nothin' that hard work won't cure," he said. "When people stop workin' they start ailin'."

"I'm sure your wife does her share," said Mama.

"No she don't," he said. "She's takin' to lyin' abed. Says her belly aches. I told her this mornin', I get a bellyache just lookin' at her."

"Why, Mr. Schwartz!" Mama's eyes grew round. "Maybe Howard should drive out to your place and take a look at her."

"Over my dead body!" said Mr. Schwartz. "My woman is not goin' to be doctorin' for every ache and pain. I told her when we got hitched, I expected her to stay in the harness. That's the only way you're goin' to make a go of farmin' this prairie."

Grandpa was right, thought Amanda. This was one mean man.

Mama sighed. "But Mr. Schwartz! You took time off when you were sick."

"But that was different," he said. "Women is like horses. I always say it's better to put your money on a new one than try to save an old one."

Women? Like horses? Amanda couldn't believe her ears.

Mama's lips narrowed to a thin line. "Mr. Schwartz, I've never heard such talk. Howard operated on you and treated you for months. Remember?"

"You bet I remember. I remember every week when I bring potatoes and eggs and chickens and geese and the Lord knows what else to this here house. Never again!" Mr. Schwartz patted the pumpkin and said, "What do you say this is worth on my bill?"

Mama lifted the pumpkin and turned it around. "About twenty cents, Mr. Schwartz."

His eyes glittered, and he licked his lips. "How about fifty cents?"

Mama handed the pumpkin back to him. "Here, Mr. Schwartz. To tell you the truth, I've become quite tired of haggling with you every time you pay your bill. I'd appreciate it if you'd pay cash at the office the way most people do."

Hooray for Mama! thought Amanda.

Mr. Schwartz glared at Mama. "One thing I can't stand is an uppity woman." He turned and stomped away.

Mama's face grew red and her eyes turned dark and wild. "Oh!" she said under her breath. "Oh!" Then she picked up a tea towel and whipped it across the back of a chair.

Amanda spoke in a near whisper. "May I go to Louise's?" Mama closed her eyes and nodded.

Amanda dashed out the door and ran the block to her best friend's house. She had to hurry if she wanted to keep Mazda.

In the Spriggses' back yard, Louise pointed to an old doghouse nearly buried in tall, dry weeds. "How about this? We don't have a dog anymore."

"No," said Amanda. "It's too little. Mazda needs more room."

They inspected the garage, looked at the space under the back porch, and stopped at a pile of old shingles.

"Maybe we could build something out of these," said Louise.

Amanda shook her head. "No. There isn't time." Then Amanda pointed to a tiny gray building half hidden behind a leafless lilac clump. "What's that?"

Louise giggled. "Don't you know what that is, Amanda?"

They climbed through the bushes, and Louise opened the squeaky, sagging door. Amanda knew when she saw the bench with two big holes on top. Lying on the floor, a torn, yellowed catalogue flapped in the breeze.

"Does anyone ever use it?"

"Can't you tell, Amanda? It doesn't even stink! Our house has had an inside bathroom for ages. My daddy was going to tear it down, but he hasn't gotten around to it yet."

Amanda said, "What if he tears it down and finds Mazda in here?"

"He won't. He's too busy fixing the roof."

"I don't want Mazda to fall into those holes." Amanda clapped her hands. "I've got it! Let's cover them with those old shingles."

Louise jumped up and down. "I'll get a hammer and some nails from the garage."

Amanda placed shingles over the holes and nailed them down. Louise brought a tin cup of water from the house and put it in the corner for Mazda.

"Now I'll have to bring Mazda over here without getting caught," said Amanda.

"I'll help," said Louise.

On the way to the chicken pen, Amanda stopped. "Mama might see us from the kitchen. I'll go in and find out where she is."

"Good idea," said Louise.

When she opened the door, Amanda heard the sound of the sewing machine treadle. She peeked into the dining room where Mama sat, stitching Margaret's new recital dress. Then Amanda tiptoed out of the house.

"We're in luck, Louise."

They cornered Mazda, and Amanda picked him up gently. He didn't make a sound.

"Let's run," whispered Amanda.

Amanda and Louise were dashing down the alley as fast as they could, when Amanda heard a voice behind them.

"Where are you going with my fighting cock?"

They stopped and turned around. What was Jack doing in the alley? Amanda wondered. She felt her face grow hot. She hated to think about what it looked like.

"Why aren't you at the store?" asked Amanda.

He held up a large paper sack. "Maybe I have a delivery to make." He walked up to them. "No kiddin'. I'm curious. Whatta ya gonna do with that rooster?"

"What do you care?" said Amanda in her snootiest voice.

"Who said I cared?" Jack winked and smiled at her. Then he walked ahead without looking back.

"He's cute," said Louise.

Amanda's feet and legs felt as if they were turning to jelly. She stood rooted to the spot.

"What's the matter, Amanda?" asked Louise. "Your face is as red as a cranberry." Then she giggled. "You like him, don't you? What's his name?"

"I do not like him," lied Amanda in a shrill voice. "His name is Jack. C'mon. Let's hide Mazda."

When the girls set Mazda down in his new home, he squawked, and when they shut the door, he screamed, "BWAWK! BWAWK!"

"Shhhh! Be quiet, Mazda!" said Amanda. "Louise, what'll I say when they ask me where he is?"

"Maybe they won't miss him."

Amanda swallowed. "I don't want to be there when Hattie comes."

"Why don't you have supper over here?"

"Good. I'll call home."

Then from somewhere above them, a man's voice said, "If you turned him over to me, I could save you a lot of trouble."

Amanda gasped. There stood Jack grinning at them through the alley side of the lilac branches.

Louise giggled.

Jack went on, "He'd have a good home in the country and wouldn't have to live in a lousy toilet."

A lousy toilet! His words shocked Amanda. She felt her face burn scarlet. Louise clapped her hands over her mouth.

"Go away and leave us alone!" shouted Amanda.

"Okay, okay. I was just trying to make you a reasonable offer." Jack walked to the alley and turned around. "If you ever change your mind, let me know."

After the evening meal, Mrs. Spriggs said, "You did real well to clean your plate, Amanda."

"Thanks for the supper, Mrs. Spriggs."

Before she went home, Amanda crawled through the lilac branches and poked a salmon cake through a wide crack in the splintery door of Mazda's new home. "Here's your supper, Mazda. I'll see you tomorrow."

In her own back yard, Amanda shivered in the cool night air and stared into the chicken pen. Moonlight threw fence shadows on the bare ground. Amanda knew the coop was empty because of the dead silence. She was afraid to go into the house, but go she must.

Mama and Daddy were having a cup of coffee in the kitchen.

"Hello, Amanda," said Mama. "How was your supper?"

"All right. We had salmon. What did you have?"

"Chicken and dumplings," said Daddy, "and it was delicious."

"You'd better do your homework, dear," said Mama. "Margaret finished hers some time ago."

"Sure, Mama." Margaret the Perfect always did everything ahead of time. Even when they had two extra days off for Thanksgiving.

Amanda heard Margaret practicing her recital piece in their bedroom, so she picked up her books and sat down at the dining room table. Why, she wondered, hadn't Mama and Daddy asked any questions about Mazda? When she opened her arithmetic book, the talking started. She strained to hear what her parents were saying, but she couldn't understand a word. Margaret's violin was making a lot of noise. Amanda moved to the side of the table nearest the kitchen. They weren't talking about her at all. They were talking about Mr. Schwartz. As she listened, Amanda stared at the pieces of cloth on the table; odd red shapes folded in tan tissue paper, which would soon be Margaret's recital dress.

Mama's voice trembled. "He compared women to horses! Oh, Howard! It was just too awful to repeat. His wife is ill, and he acted as though she weren't worth saving. I'm frightened for her. Maybe you should go see her."

Amanda shuddered. Mr. Schwartz was terrible — and creepy. Maybe Mama was so upset by him that she didn't notice Mazda was gone. But that was stretching hope too far.

"Did he ask me to come?" asked Daddy.

"No, Howard. When I suggested it, he said, 'Over my dead body.'"

"Well, then, I can't go, Martha. Someone has to call me first."

"Do you mean to tell me, Howard, that you can't stop in to see someone even if you know a cruel husband is refusing to call a doctor for his sick wife?"

"Martha, I don't know any such thing," said Daddy.

"I'm sure if Mrs. Schwartz is very ill, either she or Mr. Schwartz will call me."

Amanda agreed with Mama. She thought Daddy ought to go see Mrs. Schwartz. When the talking stopped, Amanda's hands turned to ice.

Daddy came into the dining room and stood by Amanda. "How's the homework coming, Little Kitten?" He patted her shoulder.

"Fine, Daddy."

"You'd better finish soon," Mama called from the kitchen. "It's about time to get ready for bed."

Amanda finished her homework, brushed her teeth, and put on her pajamas. No questions! No mention of Mazda!

In bed, Margaret turned to Amanda and whispered, "Where'd you hide your rooster?"

"What do you mean?" asked Amanda.

"I mean, where did you hide him?"

"Did you notice?"

"Well, I'm not blind," said Margaret.

"Did anyone else notice?"

"They're not blind either. Where'd you hide him?"

"I can't tell."

Margaret yawned and turned over. She was soon asleep, but Amanda stayed awake. After a time, she heard Mama and Daddy talking in their bedroom. Since a closed door was all that separated their rooms, she heard every word.

"Now, Martha," said Daddy, "there's nothing wrong with trying to save a life. I do it myself occasionally."

"But Howard, she disobeyed me."

"You're right there, Martha, but to tell the truth, I'd think less of her if she didn't try to save her pet."

After several seconds, Mama spoke. "Well, Howard, it's probably best to say nothing to her now. I wonder where she hid him?"

"I'm sure he'll turn up," said Daddy. "Then we can decide what to do about it."

Amanda heaved a great sigh. It was wonderful to know that she and Mazda were both safe.

❧ *Chapter 6* ❧

*A*s she had done every evening for the past three weeks, Amanda opened the door a crack to feed Mazda. She shivered. The cold wind bit her cheeks, and her breath puffed white clouds as she spoke.

"Shame on you, Mazda! I heard you crow this morning and I heard you yesterday, too." She listened for Mazda's scratching and rustling, but heard nothing. Maybe he's sick, she thought. She opened the door a little wider and gasped. He was gone!

"AMANDA!" Mama was calling. She had to run home this minute and get ready to go to Margaret's recital. It wasn't fair. Margaret's big recital at a time like this! Her stomach churned and her heart pounded in her ears. Her eyes searched the yard for some trace of Mazda, but she saw only tall yellow grasses bending in the wind. The sun was going down, and through the Spriggses' kitchen window, Amanda saw Louise at the table with her parents. Louise would surely know what happened, but this was no time to knock at their door. She'd phone Louise when she got home.

"Thank goodness you're here, Amanda." Mama clamped a hot curling iron onto a lock of Margaret's hair, rolled it up, and held it until the iron cooled. "You'll just have time to change your clothes, and don't forget to wash your face and hands." She hung the iron into the oil lamp chimney to heat up for the next curl.

Amanda looked in the mirror after putting on the pink striped dress that used to be Margaret's. It was too large and made her look thinner than ever. She opened a cigar box under Listerine's bed and found the frayed hair ribbon that went with the dress. Under the ribbon lay a gold coin Grandpa had given her on her last birthday. She lifted it out and turned it over in her hand. Could it be a lucky charm? With Mazda missing, she needed luck. Grandpa would just die if he could hear her thoughts. The one thing he hated more than Mr. Schwartz was superstition. With a twinge of guilt, she decided to give it a try. She dropped the gold piece into her coat pocket and went into the front room where the others waited. She couldn't call Louise now. Everyone would hear. Amanda's stomach ached with worry.

Margaret knelt on the floor and opened her violin case. She plucked the strings and loosened her bow. She looked pretty in her new red dress, but her face wore a solemn expression.

"What if I forget my piece, Mama?"

Mama's reflection smiled at Margaret as she put on her hat in front of the mirror. "You won't, dear. You've practiced and practiced."

Margaret ran to Daddy and threw her arms around him. "I'm scared."

Daddy patted her on the back. "Fear's not always bad, Princess. It sometimes helps you do a good job."

"I'm scared, too." Amanda ran over and hugged Daddy.

"What on earth are you frightened for, Little Kitten?"

"For Margaret." Amanda knew her answer was only half true. She'd caught herself lying a lot lately — lies covering the hidden Mazda and those embarrassing feelings about Jack. Secrets were squeezing in on her, crowding her, making her feel like a stranger with her own family. Amanda doubted Margaret had ever had a secret in her whole life. She was too perfect. But Hal might have secrets.

Hal sighed and looked out the window. "Do I have to go?"

"Certainly," said Daddy. "We all have to be there to cheer Margaret on."

Margaret giggled. "Daddy! It's not a football game."

Hal groaned. "I wish it were." He brushed the curtain aside. "Hey! It's starting to sleet. Maybe we won't have to go after all."

Mama looked out the window. "Of course we'll go. Are you coming to the violin recital, Grandpa?"

Grandpa looked over his newspaper at Mama. "I don't have to get all dressed up and sit in the Methodist church to hear cats meowin'."

The telephone rang. Amanda jumped. Maybe it was Louise! Daddy beat her to it.

"Well, Mrs. Atkins," said Daddy, "just stay calm and

put him in a tub of cool water. I'll be over there in a few minutes."

Amanda's throat tightened. Why didn't Louise call?

After Daddy hung up, Margaret said, "Will you be able to hear me play tonight, Daddy?" Her voice quavered.

Daddy put his arms around Margaret. "Marty Atkins's boy just had a convulsion. If it isn't serious, I'll come as soon as I can. Now, Princess, if I can't get there in time, just remember that I want you to play as well as you possibly can. I hope you understand, my dear."

Margaret swallowed hard. "Sure, Daddy."

Daddy picked up his case. "Coats on, everyone. I'll drop you off on my way to the Atkinses'."

In the car, Amanda sat in the back seat between Hal and Margaret, her feet on Daddy's doctor bag. It was too late to call Louise now. Amanda told herself that on such a cold night, Louise had probably moved Mazda to a warmer place. But where? What warmer place was there? The house? Mrs. Spriggs would have a fit.

Mama handed Hal a plate wrapped in waxed paper — cookies for the party after the program. "Hold these, please, Hal." Then she looked at Amanda. "What are you doing, dear?"

"Tying my gold piece in my handkerchief."

"Oh, Amanda, you shouldn't have brought your gold piece. You might lose it."

"I won't." Amanda stuffed the tied-up coin into her coat pocket and rubbed it as she silently chanted,

"Coin, coin, bring me luck. Bring me luck, oh coin, coin!"

In the church hallway, the people around the coatrack brushed tiny ice beads off their hats and shoulders.

Mama saw Mrs. Harpool. "Why, Tess! It's good to see you."

"It's a bad night," said Mrs. Harpool. "A real bad night. I tell you, though, I'd walk through flood water to hear that Dorothy Thornhill play. You mark my word. She'll put Prairie Bend on the map one of these days." Mrs. Harpool lowered her voice. "I can't say much for her sister Virginia, though. If you ask me, she's turning out to be a bad apple."

Why, Amanda wondered, would Mrs. Harpool call beautiful, friendly Virginia Thornhill a "bad apple"? She made her sound so rotten.

"Excuse me, Tess," said Mama. "Hal, will you take the cookies to the basement, please?" Margaret went to get some programs from Mr. Gilly, but Amanda stayed with Mama, hoping to hear more about Virginia.

Mrs. Harpool said, "Haven't you heard about it, Martha? Everyone in town is talking about the way Virginia carries on with that young man her daddy hired."

Jack! Amanda's thoughts whirled. Jack and Virginia! As romantic a couple as she could imagine. If only she were as old as Virginia, and as pretty! What did "carrying on" mean? She'd ask. "Mrs. Harpool, what does —"

Mama interrupted by exclaiming, "Why, Tess! Just

look at all the people coming!" She pushed Amanda toward the auditorium. "Excuse us. We'd better go in or we won't find good seats."

Amanda counted the people coming in the door. Only three.

Amanda, Hal, and Mama sat down on a long, slippery pew. Margaret sat up front with the others on the program and kept looking back. Amanda knew she was checking to see if Daddy had come. She studied the faded purple names on the mimeographed sheet and spotted Margaret's third from the top. Margaret had told Amanda that the best musicians were last. The very last name on the program was Dorothy Thornhill. She was Mr. Gilly's star pupil.

Mr. and Mrs. Thornhill, Virginia, and her little brother Billy, sat in front of the Albees. They looked back and smiled. Amanda thought Virginia looked especially lovely in her blue silk dress. Mrs. Harpool must be a cranky witch to call her a "bad apple." Did "carrying on" with Jack mean kissing? What was so terrible about that? She might like to "carry on" with Jack herself if she were a whole lot older.

Someone pushed a key down on the piano, and the crowd hushed. Sadie Blankenship, who was in the second grade, tuned her violin. She played a piece called "Glow Worm" all the way through without any mistakes that Amanda could hear, but she squeaked and squawked a lot. When she finished, the Blankenships, who sat behind the Albees, clapped the longest and the loudest.

Margaret looked back again. Daddy still hadn't

come. Amanda thought about Mazda. If Louise's mother had found him, what had she been doing in that old outhouse? Louise said no one ever used it. Could her mother have cooked Mazda? When she saw them sitting at the table, they could have been eating Mazda Soup! The thought made Amanda's stomach, which up to now had calmed down a little, roll and churn. Could her best friend actually sit at the table and eat Mazda Soup? Amanda didn't think so, but still . . .

Elizabeth Tuttle, who was in the third grade, had just finished playing Minuet in G, and Margaret was next. Amanda's hands turned icy, and her mouth felt dry. Margaret looked back, but Daddy still wasn't there. When Margaret stepped up on the stage, Amanda couldn't look. She had two worries now. Mazda and Margaret. Her head started to ache along with her stomach. She untied her gold piece and turned it around in her hand. It was pretty, but was it magic? She placed the coin in the middle of her handkerchief and twisted the ends into a column. Then she wondered if covering a lucky charm reduced its power. What if Grandpa could hear her thoughts? Out of respect for him, she left the gold piece in the handkerchief. When Amanda glanced at Hal, she saw that he'd slouched down until his knees touched the pew in front. He was staring at his folded hands, and looked miserable. If Margaret forgot her piece, it would be embarrassing, but, on the other hand, it would show Mama and Daddy that Margaret wasn't perfect. Then Amanda heard a familiar sound. Margaret was playing.

When Amanda peeked, she noticed that her sister looked pretty up there on stage. With her golden hair curled and falling on her shoulders, Amanda thought Margaret stood a better chance than she did of looking like Virginia Thornhill someday. And surprise! Her playing sounded better than it ever had at home.

Before Margaret finished, Daddy came in and sat down beside Amanda. He smiled, put his arm around her, and squeezed her shoulder. When Margaret looked out at the applauding audience and saw Daddy, she grinned. Amanda knew it was wrong, but she felt disappointed that Daddy got there in time to hear her. Amanda leaned over and whispered in Daddy's ear.

"May we go home now?"

"No, Little Kitten. We must stay and hear the others."

Amanda counted the rest of the names on the program. Ten! She was too nervous to sit through ten violin pieces. "May I go to the bathroom, Daddy?"

He whispered, "Do you know where it is?"

"I'll find it." Amanda tiptoed into the hall. She'd find a telephone and call Louise. Surely this church had a telephone. Amanda saw a stairway and went down into a large room where ladies were arranging cups and plates on a long table. Then she passed an open door. When she looked in, she saw a tall, black telephone standing on a desk. Amanda went in and closed the door.

"I'm sorry," the operator said, "but that line is busy."

After a trip to the ladies' room, Amanda saw a young

man walking down the hall in front of her. His back was turned, so he didn't see her. And she couldn't see his face, but somehow she knew it was Jack. He turned into an unlit hallway and disappeared. What was he doing down here? she wondered. Why wasn't he going upstairs to the recital?

Amanda went back to the telephone. Still busy. "Darn!" she muttered. If she stayed down here much longer, someone would come looking for her. She just had to ask Louise about Mazda. She tried once more. No luck. She tiptoed upstairs and took her seat.

The program had moved on to the more advanced pupils now and sounded better. When Dorothy Thornhill finally took the stage, the audience applauded even before she played.

"Why are they clapping now, Daddy?" asked Amanda.

"It's because Dorothy Thornhill is so good. Listen and you'll see why."

The audience sank into a deep silence when Dorothy played. Her body swayed and her fingers flew. Amanda found it hard to believe that such beautiful music could come from a violin. The sound was so lovely that Amanda actually forgot about Mazda for a few minutes. When Dorothy finished, the applause roared on and on, until she announced her encore.

After the recital, the Albees joined the others in the church basement. Mrs. Harpool took Mama aside and started talking very fast. It was probably good Grandpa didn't come, thought Amanda. He'd go on and on about the wireless, and everybody'd think he was crazy.

Amanda ran over to where Mama and Mrs. Harpool stood hoping to hear more about Jack and Virginia.

The feathers on Mrs. Harpool's hat bobbed up and down. "I heard it from someone who should know. Walter Thornhill told that young man, 'If I catch you with Virginia again, I'll see that you leave town and never come back.' Walter thinks he's not classy enough for his daughter."

Amanda looked around, but she didn't see Virginia. Where was she? Billy and Mr. and Mrs. Thornhill stood together at the other end of the room talking to Dorothy. Daddy was with some people Amanda didn't know, and Hal and Margaret were eating cookies and talking to Mr. Gilly.

"Excuse us, Tess," said Mama. "We should talk to some of the others before they leave." Amanda noticed that whenever Mama heard gossip, she turned away or changed the subject, so Amanda seldom got to hear anything exciting. They walked over to where Dorothy Thornhill stood.

"You were magnificent," said Mama to Dorothy. "The star of the evening." Mama hugged her and patted her on the back. "Everyone in Prairie Bend loves you for sharing your special gift."

Across the room, Amanda saw Mr. Gilly talking with Mrs. Harpool. He mopped his red face with a large white handkerchief. Amanda gasped when she remembered her own handkerchief. The gold piece! It was twisted inside! She must have left it on the pew upstairs! Losing a good-luck piece was a terrible sign. She had to find it!

Amanda ran up the steps and felt the wall for a light switch, but couldn't find one. As she tiptoed through the dark church, the street lamp shining through the stained glass window threw colored patterns on the pews. Shadows danced on the walls as a tree swayed in the wind. Amanda shuddered. This was scary. It was like looking for treasure in a cave. Feeling her way through the dark, she found the pew where she'd sat, and lifted a program off the seat. The twisted handkerchief was underneath, just where she'd left it, and the gold coin was inside. Finding the lucky charm could be a sign — a sign that Louise found Mazda and was right this minute putting him back in his house. Amanda snatched it up, kissed it, and ran into the dim hallway. She found her coat hanging on the rack and dropped the gold piece into the pocket.

Then she heard breathing and shuffling noises. She tiptoed toward the sound and stared into a shadow. A few feet away, stood Virginia Thornhill and Jack with their arms around each other. Amanda felt her knees turn watery and her face grow hot. Embarrassed, she ran away, stumbling over a brace on the coatrack. She fell forward, toppling a metal wastebasket. The clatter rang in her ears. Then she felt herself being jerked up by the collar. She tried to get away from him, but Jack held onto her.

"Little spies oughta be spanked," he said. "If you tell anyone what you saw, you'll be plenty sorry. You hear?"

Virginia shrank farther into the shadow.

"I wasn't spying," said Amanda. "I was just putting my money in my coat pocket."

"Tell that to the birds," said Jack.

"It's true." Amanda's knee hurt terribly. She looked down and saw that it was bleeding.

Jack yanked at her collar again.

"Jack! Don't! She's just a child," said Virginia.

"Yeah, but this kid has a big mouth. She writes letters to the newspaper."

Virginia came out of the shadows. "Leave her alone, Jack."

Jack let her go. "Okay, but button your lip, kid, or no tellin' what'll happen to you."

Amanda couldn't believe that such a mix of feelings could whirl around inside her. She was frightened, embarrassed, thrilled, and jealous all at the same time.

At home, Daddy sat down and examined Amanda's knee. "How did it happen, Little Kitten?"

"I fell." It was going to be hard to keep quiet about Jack and Virginia. What did Jack mean when he said, "Button your lip, kid, or no tellin' what'll happen to you"? She had been too scared to ask what he'd had in mind. When Daddy painted her wound with iodine, Amanda tried not to cry, but she couldn't help it. As Daddy put the last strip of tape on her bandage, the doorbell rang.

A gust of cold air swept through the room as Mama held the door open.

"Why, Mrs. Spriggs! Come in."

Mrs. Spriggs! Amanda felt dizzy. She might faint.

"I hate coming here at this time of night," said Mrs.

Spriggs. "I tried to call earlier, but you were out, and I didn't want to bother you at supper time —"

"It's all right," said Daddy. "We just came home. What can we do for you?"

Mrs. Spriggs sighed. "Well, at five o'clock this evening, a sheriff's deputy knocked at the door, and I was fined."

"Fined!" cried Mama. "Whatever for?"

Amanda knew what for and grabbed the table to steady herself.

"For keeping your rooster in our outhouse." Mrs. Spriggs blew her nose. "I've never been so embarrassed in my life! The neighbors heard him crow and called the sheriff. I had to pay three dollars!"

"Mercy!" Mama clapped a hand over her mouth.

"After the deputy came," said Mrs. Spriggs, "we tied the rooster up in a gunnysack and stuck him in the basement till we could bring him over here. I left him out there on your front porch. He can't get away. He's still in the gunnysack."

Amanda swallowed. So this is what Daddy had meant when he said, "I'm sure he'll turn up."

Daddy looked down at Amanda. "Young lady, what do you know about this?"

Amanda felt her insides drop to her feet and freeze into blocks so heavy that even Mr. Cox couldn't have lifted them. A circle of eyes captured her as she made her confession.

Then when she went out on the front porch to move Mazda to the back yard, Amanda thought there had been some mistake. She looked for the gunnysack, but there was none. No Mazda. Nothing. The porch was bare except for the swing hanging from its ceiling chains and swaying in the breeze. Hardly able to believe her eyes, Amanda couldn't stop the tears when she ran inside and cried, "He's gone!"

"But that's impossible!" exclaimed Mrs. Spriggs. "I left him out there myself a few minutes ago!" Mrs. Spriggs went out to check and came in with eyes the size of doorknobs. "You're right, Amanda. He's gone. I don't understand it. He was in a bag with SUNSHINE FEEDS printed on it."

Daddy, Hal, and Amanda went outside and walked all around the house. Then they searched the back yard. No feed sack. No Mazda.

When they came in, Daddy said, "Amanda, I hope this isn't another one of your tricks. You didn't hide him again, did you?"

"No. Honest!" Amanda shook with sobs. Daddy didn't trust her anymore.

"How strange," said Mama.

Daddy took Amanda in his arms and patted her back. "Well, there are a lot of hungry people around these days, Little Kitten. Maybe some poor family needed him."

"No! No!" Amanda wailed. How could Daddy say such a thing! Kidnaped or stolen? Yes! But eaten? Never! She'd promised Grandma she'd take good care of him. She'd promised! Besides, she loved him!

Later, as Amanda tried to keep the bed covers from touching her knee, she gasped with dry sobs. The tears had been cried out. She couldn't decide which part of this horrible evening had been the worst. It was one terrible thing after another. Mama and Daddy said she had to pay back Mrs. Spriggs's fine. Three whole dollars! It would take the rest of her life to earn that much! Then at bedtime the most awful hurt feeling came over her when Daddy put his arms around Margaret and said, "Princess, your mother and I are proud of you. You stood there in front of a big crowd and did your best."

Amanda wouldn't dare tell him, of course, but Grandpa would be pleased to know that his gold piece was not a lucky charm.

She made up her mind about one thing, though. She'd do everything she possibly could to find Mazda.

❦ *Chapter 7* ❦

"*G*et out of my yard." A heavyset old woman in a purple bathrobe struggled down her back steps. "Get out!"

"Oh, oh!" Amanda pulled at Louise's sleeve. The two of them scooted through the gate and dashed down the street.

The old woman yelled, "I'll teach you to snoop in my yard!"

Louise muttered, "Cranky old witch!" and ran on ahead.

Amanda stopped and turned around. The old woman stood on the sidewalk and shook her cane at them.

"We were looking for my lost rooster," cried Amanda. "Have you seen him?"

"Humph! Lost rooster!" scoffed the old woman. "That beats all the stories I ever heard." She hobbled back through her gate.

As they walked toward home, Amanda kicked a pebble along the brick sidewalk. "Darn! Darn!"

"Why don't we give up?" asked Louise. "We'll never find him."

"We will too!" said Amanda. "And we still have the east side to do. You promised to help." Amanda's words sounded hollow even to herself. Louise is probably right, she thought.

"I'm tired of looking, Amanda. A whole week, and we haven't found one chicken — let alone Mazda. Besides, it's too cold." Louise blew on her hands.

Ever since Mazda had disappeared, a suspicion had grown in Amanda's mind about a certain person who could have stolen him, but she hoped it wasn't so. It would be a lot simpler to find him in somebody's back yard. If her guess was right, it might take more courage than she had to get him back. Still, the thought nibbled away at her zest for yard searching.

"I have an idea," said Amanda. "Come with me."

"Where are we going?"

"You'll see."

They ran several blocks, then Amanda stopped across the street from Prairie Bend High School.

"Sit here, Louise." Amanda patted the curb beside her.

"What for?" Louise was panting.

"I want to ask Virginia Thornhill something. She'll be coming out that door in a few minutes.

"Why Virginia Thornhill?" asked Louise.

"She may know where Mazda is."

"How would she know?"

Questions, questions! Amanda was sorry she'd asked Louise to come along. "Her boyfriend may have taken him. He works in her dad's store."

"You mean Jack?"

"Uh-huh." Amanda hated to talk about Jack in front

of Louise. She teased. With a stick, she drew an outline of Mazda in the street dust. "Remember when he saw us hide Mazda? And he asked to take him? He's always wanted him."

"Then why don't you just go to Thornhill's and ask him?"

Amanda sighed. "I don't want to. Besides, I don't think he'd tell me."

Louise giggled. "You like him, don't you?"

"I don't know whether I do or not. Stop talking about it." Amanda hadn't set foot in Thornhill's store since she first saw Jack there, and she hoped she wouldn't have to — especially since the night of the recital. She could still remember how it felt when Jack grabbed her by the collar.

"Hey!" cried Louise. "The doors are opening! What does she look like, Amanda?"

"Real pretty. Blond." Amanda watched the students spill out from the big double doors. She spotted Virginia with several others. At the bottom of the steps, she broke from the group and started for home.

"Let's catch up with her," whispered Amanda. They crossed the street and followed her. Then Amanda called out, "Hi, Virginia."

Virginia stopped and turned around. "Oh, hello, Amanda."

Amanda walked up beside Virginia. "This is Louise."

"Hello, Louise."

Amanda swallowed hard. It wasn't easy to talk about Jack. She took a deep breath. "Virginia . . ." She paused. "Where does Jack live?"

Virginia stopped and searched Amanda's face with her eyes. "Why do you want to know that, Amanda?"

"He may have my rooster."

Virginia's mouth smiled but her eyes didn't. There were no crinkles at the corners.

"Does he have my rooster?" asked Amanda.

"Amanda, I don't know."

"Then tell me where he lives." If she knew that, Amanda thought, she could just go there and steal Mazda back and never have to face Jack at all.

Virginia's voice shook, and her eyes filled with tears. "I can't tell you that."

"Don't you know where he lives?" Amanda couldn't believe that Virginia didn't know.

"I just can't talk about it, that's all." Virginia hurried on, leaving Amanda and Louise behind.

"I wonder what she meant by that?" asked Louise.

"Something's bothering her. She isn't going to tell us," said Amanda.

"Looks like you'll have to ask Jack himself," said Louise.

"Will you go with me?" Amanda's voice trembled. Having Louise along would give her courage.

Louise shook her head. "Don't have time. Have to be home by four."

Amanda gulped. "I'll see you later, then." As she watched Louise run home, it was all she could do to keep from changing her mind and racing to catch up with her. But if she hoped to find Mazda, she had to follow her hunch, so she went downtown.

Amanda walked around the block twice to work up

the courage to go into Thornhill's store. Then she peeked in the window to see if Jack was there. He wasn't. Maybe he was in the back room, she thought. Instead, she saw Grandpa inside talking to Mr. Thornhill. Jack wouldn't dare be mean to her with Grandpa standing right there. She went in.

"Well, look who's here!" said Mr. Thornhill. "Your granddaddy and I were talkin' politics, and in walks the apple of his eye."

"Hello, Mr. Thornhill. Hi, Grandpa." When Amanda skipped under Grandpa's outstretched arm, she felt safe from Jack or anyone else.

Grandpa drew her close. "What do you think o' this Indian Fighter o' mine, Walter?"

Mr. Thornhill's eyes twinkled. "That's a spunky one. Takes after you, I think. You won't believe this, but she's the one who put the bee in my bonnet about running for mayor."

Amanda grinned. "Are you going to run for mayor, Mr. Thornhill? Really?"

"Well, I've been thinkin' about it."

"Be a fine public service," said Grandpa. "I don't like the way Butler's been cozying up to people like Lester Schwartz. Hope you run, Walter. I'll do everything I can to help you."

"I will too," shouted Amanda. Maybe she could deliver handbills like Davy did when his dad ran! Mr. Thornhill for mayor! And all because she suggested it. He had listened to her — a kid!

"Thanks." Mr. Thornhill's eyes crinkled at the corners the way Virginia's always had before today.

Amanda was so thrilled about Mr. Thornhill's running for mayor, that she almost forgot her errand. Was Jack in the stockroom? She didn't want to ask. Her courage was fading. She'd walk home with Grandpa and come back another time.

"Are you going home, Grandpa?"

"Nope. I'm on my way over to meet some o' the fellas at the Wild Goose." The Wild Goose Cafe! The Albee children weren't allowed to go there because it had a back room where people sometimes drank whiskey and played poker. Amanda knew Grandpa would never drink or gamble, but he wouldn't be afraid to talk to people who did.

Grandpa opened the door and stopped as if he suddenly remembered something. "Walter, what happened to that young fella you had in here?"

Mr. Thornhill's face grew sober. "Jack? He doesn't work here anymore."

Doesn't work here anymore! The words throbbed in Amanda's ears. Fear for Mazda prickled the back of her neck.

"Didn't steal from ya, did he?" asked Grandpa.

"Oh, no, no, no. Nothing like that," said Mr. Thornhill. "Good to see you, Mr. Albee." Mr. Thornhill looked down at Amanda. "Now, young lady, what can I do for you?"

Amanda's thoughts erased Mr. Thornhill's voice. Jack was gone! Fired? Because of Virginia? She could come in here now any time she wanted. That part of it felt good, but suppose he'd left town with Mazda! She had to ask where Jack lived!

Mr. Thornhill laughed. "What's the matter, Amanda? Cat got your tongue?"

Amanda smiled. She had to say something, but she didn't want Mr. Thornhill to know she came in here just to ask about Jack. "Do you still have those roller skates?" She pointed to the counter. "I remember they were right up there."

Mr. Thornhill stroked his chin. "Hmmm. Looks like someone bought 'em."

"Do you have any more?"

He reached down and put another box of skates up on display. "Are these what you had in mind?"

She nodded. "Who bought the others?" She hoped it was Mama or Daddy. She'd hinted enough.

"Oh, now I can't go around tellin' everything I know. We all have to keep a few secrets, especially now with Christmas just around the corner."

Amanda smiled. There was no graceful way to bring it up. She'd just ask. "Mr. Thornhill, do you know where Jack lives?" Amanda's scalp tingled and her feet felt heavy. She could feel a blush coming.

Mr. Thornhill didn't seem to notice. "Last I heard, he was rentin' a room from Mrs. Schooler down on Tenth."

Mrs. Schooler's on Tenth! She knew where that was. She ran to the door, then turned and said, "I hope you get to be mayor, Mr. Thornhill!"

Amanda ran the five blocks to Mrs. Schooler's house. She knew the way. Mama had often sent her to Mrs. Schooler's with napkins and dress ruffles to be hemstitched; she owned a machine that did quick fancy-work. But Mrs. Schooler was better known in Prairie Bend for her piano playing at the movie theater. During the silent films, she accompanied the whole show, but now, with the talkies, she played just before the picture started. And she rented out rooms in her big frame house.

Amanda twisted the fancy iron key, and the doorbell scraped and jangled. She loved that sound and was about to ring again when the door opened. Amanda was disappointed to see that Mrs. Schooler wasn't dressed up in one of the evening gowns she wore at the theater. Show time wasn't till seven. It was only about four, and she was wearing a cotton housedress. The creases in Mrs. Schooler's wrinkled face deepened as she smiled.

"Hello, Amanda. What can I do for you today?"

"Does Jack live here?" Amanda's voice had thinned to a half-whisper.

"Jack who?"

Amanda's face grew hot. Odd not to know his last name. She'd never thought about it. He must have one. "I don't know. He used to work at Thornhill's."

"Oh, yes. That Jack. He moved out last Thursday."

Moved out? Amanda's stomach lurched. "Where did he go?"

"I don't really know. Is there something I can help you with?"

"Did he have a rooster?"

"Ummmm, noooo." Then Mrs. Schooler studied the ceiling as if she was trying to remember something. She bit her lip and looked down at Amanda. "Come to

77

think of it, that gunnysack could have had a rooster in it. I didn't look."

"A gunnysack!" Amanda felt she was stretching for a kite string just out of reach. "Where is it?"

"Oh, it's gone now," said Mrs. Schooler. "But last Thursday, when I came out to get the morning paper, I heard a rustling sound under the porch. When I looked, I saw a moving gunnysack. I thought at the time —"

"Did the gunnysack have SUNSHINE FEEDS printed on it?"

"Why, yes. I believe it did. Sunshine Feeds. Yes."

"That was Mazda!"

Mrs. Schooler smiled. "Mazda?"

"My pet rooster. My grandma gave him to me."

Mrs. Schooler went on, "Well, I went in the house to ask if anyone knew what it was doing there. I never allow pets. But then I got busy and forgot it. And later that day, Jack moved out. Then when I checked under the porch again, the gunnysack was gone."

"That was my pet rooster!" shouted Amanda. "He has it! Where did he move?" Please! Please! she wished, let it be close by!

"I don't know. All he said was, 'I'm moving to the country.' I asked what I should do with his mail, and he said he wouldn't be getting any." Mrs. Schooler smiled. "I'm afraid I haven't been very helpful."

The country! The country! The word bounced and echoed in Amanda's head. What did it mean? A short walk from town? Or someplace miles and miles from

Prairie Bend? Amanda ran all the way to Louise's house and pounded on the door.

When Louise saw Amanda, she said, "What's wrong?"

"Everything," said Amanda. "Jack has Mazda, and he's moved to the country, and nobody knows where." Amanda told Louise what Mr. Thornhill and Mrs. Schooler had said.

"What are you going to do now?" asked Louise.

"Find out where Jack lives."

"How?"

"When he comes to town, ask him."

Louise sighed. "Suppose he never comes to town? You may never see him again."

Amanda's jaw muscles tightened. "All country people come to town if they live anywhere around here. And most of them go downtown on Saturday night. That's where we'll have to look for him, Louise. Downtown on Saturday night!"

"You're crazy, Amanda. Our folks'll never let us go by ourselves on Saturday night."

"I'll have someone take us. We'll find a way, Louise!"

On Saturday night, Mama and Daddy couldn't go downtown. They were invited to the Latimers'. Grandpa was going to a political meeting at the north end of town. And Hal had been asked to a party. That left Margaret, who was too young to take Amanda anywhere at night.

After Saturday's supper, Amanda was looking out

79

the living room window, wondering whether a sneak downtown would be worth a spanking, when the telephone rang. It was Louise.

"Guess what, Amanda! My folks decided to go shopping tonight and will take us downtown. Do you still want to go?"

"Do I want to go?" yelled Amanda. "You bet!" Good! thought Amanda. Mrs. Spriggs must not be too mad at her anymore.

Mr. Spriggs parked their old black Ford in front of Carney's Variety Store. When they got out, Mrs. Spriggs spoke to the girls. "Meet us back here at nine-thirty. And if you see us in any of the stores, just go somewhere else."

Louise giggled. "What are you going to buy, Mama?"

"Never mind," said Mrs. Spriggs. "You may find out on Christmas and you may not. It all depends." Mr. and Mrs. Spriggs went into the variety store.

Amanda patted her coat pockets. She had Grandpa's magnifying glass in one and a notepad and pencil in the other. She was ready to do serious detective work like Sherlock Holmes or Nancy Drew.

"Let's sit in the car and watch people go by," said Amanda, "and if Jack shows up, I'll run out and ask him some questions." Amanda and Louise sat and watched the crowds of farmers and their families as they walked along Main Street and went in and out of stores. They hadn't watched very long, when Virginia Thornhill hurried through the crowds. A light snow began to fall. Amanda noticed how lovely Virginia looked in her dark winter coat with its turned up collar. Snowflakes sprinkled her shoulders and sparkled on the brim of her hat. But her eyes looked the way they did the other afternoon, serious, somehow.

Amanda nudged Louise. "Let's follow her. She might be meeting Jack."

They got out of the car and stayed far enough behind Virginia so she wouldn't notice them. They watched as Virginia turned the corner and bought a ticket at the Strand Theatre. The blinking lights above the cashier's booth said, JAMES CAGNEY IN PUBLIC ENEMY.

"Let's go to the picture show," said Amanda.

"But she's going by herself! If she was meeting Jack they'd go in together."

"Not if she's meeting him in secret. He could be waiting for her inside."

"That's crazy," said Louise. "What if he's not in there?"

"We'll get to see the show." Amanda felt she had nothing to lose. She loved the movies almost as much as she did animals.

Louise laughed. "You're right. I have money. How about you?"

"Sure." Amanda held up a dime.

They waited until Virginia went in, then Amanda asked the cashier, "When is the show over?"

"Nine-fifteen. The newsreel just started."

"Aw heck," said Amanda. "We missed Mrs. Schooler."

"Did we miss the cartoon?" asked Louise.

"No. That's next."

Amanda turned to Louise, "We'll have plenty of time. Why not?"

They paid their money, and a girl usher in a red satin costume with a gold trimmed jacket led them down an aisle with a flashlight.

"We want to sit in the back," said Amanda.

"Why?" asked Louise.

"So we can watch for you-know-who. You can't see anyone up front."

After they sat down, Amanda looked for Virginia. At first she couldn't see anything until her eyes got used to the dark. Then she saw her across the aisle in the very back row, sitting by herself.

"See, Amanda?" said Louise. "What did I tell you? She came alone!"

"Oh, well," said Amanda. "We tried. Anyway, we get to see the show."

They watched a newsreel about thousands of poor people pitching tents in Washington, D.C., so that President Hoover could see for himself how terrible it was to be poor. Then they laughed and giggled all through the Mickey Mouse cartoon. As the feature started, the usher flashed her light in the back row across the aisle. When Amanda looked up, she couldn't believe her eyes. It was Jack. He slipped in front of several people to sit down by Virginia.

"Jack just came in," Amanda whispered to Louise.

"What? You're kidding!"

Amanda pointed. "Look."

"What do we do now?" asked Louise.

"Watch. And follow them."

Halfway through the movie, Jack and Virginia got up to leave. Amanda poked Louise and said, "They're going out. Are you coming with me?"

"I want to see the rest of the movie."

"Meet you back here after the show," said Amanda. She hid inside the drinking fountain niche and watched Jack open the heavy outside door. He looked down the street both ways and nodded to Virginia, who was standing behind the cashier's stand.

"The coast is clear," he said.

Outside the theater, Amanda saw them walk away and turn off on a side street. At the corner, she stood behind a cedar bush and watched. The snow had stopped, but Amanda shivered with the cold. Jack opened the door of a parked truck and kissed Virginia's hair as she climbed in. Then he went around and got in on the driver's side. Had Amanda missed her chance? She waited, but they didn't go anywhere. Were they kissing? Probably. Amanda wondered what it would feel like to be kissed by Jack. Every muscle in her body seemed to go limp and her toes tingled. It was scary. She stared at the back of the truck, but she couldn't see a thing through the rear window. Should she knock on the door? Amanda's teeth chattered, partly from the cold, but mostly from fear. Jack would be mad. Maybe even madder than at the recital. She crouched down behind the bush. She had to do something! So she opened her notepad and wrote down the truck's license number. Detectives always did that. Here she was, she thought, a half a block away, and she felt too scared and embarrassed to ask him about Mazda. Mazda! How beautiful he was with his gleaming tail feathers and tall comb. How she missed holding his warm, feathery body, and feeding him, and talking to him. Not only that. He was Grandma's last gift to her. And Jack had the gall to steal him right off their front porch. How dare he do such a mean thing! Her anger grew until it seemed to burn up her fear. She didn't care how mad he got. She had to fight for what was hers. This could be her last chance.

She sprang up and ran toward the truck. But before she got there, the motor zoomed, and the tires spun on the gravel. She stopped and stared as the truck disappeared around the next corner. Did he see her? He could have.

"Shoot!" she muttered. She'd be faster and braver next time — if there was a next time. But she had his license number — 6F-4469.

❧ *Chapter 8* ❧

*C*lancy, the Latimers' Irish setter, sniffed at Amanda's oatmeal and looked up at her with sad brown eyes. Amanda stroked his head and scratched him behind the ears.

"Aren't you hungry, Clancy?" She put a sheet of tablet paper with oatmeal on it right under the dog's nose. Clancy lifted his head, and walked around to the other side of her.

"Come on, now, Clancy. Mazda used to eat it for me. And until I get him back, you're going to be my pet." Amanda set the oatmeal at Clancy's feet. Ignoring it, he sat down, gazed up at her, and swept his tail back and forth across the sidewalk.

Amanda sighed. "I don't know what I'm going to do with you, Clancy. I have to go to Daddy's office now. I'll leave that oatmeal right here. And when I come back, I want it to be all gone." She shook her finger at Clancy. "If you don't eat it, you won't grow up to be a healthy, beautiful dog!"

At Daddy's office, Lucille Weber inspected Amanda's work and said, "You'll have to rub harder to get the fingerprints off those chair arms." Lucille was Daddy's secretary, lab assistant, bookkeeper, typist, receptionist, and cleaning lady. Daddy paid her ten dollars for a six-day week, a very good wage.

It was Amanda's second Saturday helping Lucille with the office cleaning. She had ten more to go before she earned the three dollars. Of course Daddy had paid Mrs. Spriggs right away, and Amanda was working to pay Daddy back.

"Here's the Dutch Cleanser for the bathroom," said Lucille.

Amanda wrinkled her nose. "Do I have to clean the bathroom?"

Lucille smiled. "We can do it together. First, though, why don't you dust your daddy's back office while I boil his instruments?" Lucille disappeared behind the frosted glass door of the examining room.

As Amanda wiped Daddy's desk with an oily cloth, she noticed a pile of forms with CASE HISTORY printed at the tops in fat black letters. There was space for a person's name, and below that, the word DIAGNOSIS with a half-page for Daddy to fill in. Some of the sheets had just a word or two, but others had a lot of writing.

"Lucille," Amanda called, "what does 'diagnosis' mean?"

Lucille looked out and grinned at her. "It's what the doctor thinks the patient has." Then Lucille gasped and rushed to the desk. She swept the case histories into a stack and hugged them to her chest. "Whew! That would have been awful!"

"What would have been awful?" asked Amanda.

"Your father told me never to let anyone see the patients' records."

"Why?"

"They're secret." Lucille put the jagged pile face down on a tall, wooden file cabinet and placed Daddy's snowing paperweight on top of them. Then she hurried back to the examining room.

Secret! The word was excitement itself! Amanda felt drawn to the papers. She looked up and watched the paperweight's snowflakes swirl and settle on the tiny church and trees in the little glass ball. There'd be nothing wrong with taking a peek, she thought. After all, wasn't she in Daddy's own family? And didn't he often talk about his patients? She pushed Daddy's desk chair against the file cabinet and stood on it. When Amanda lifted the paperweight, she set off a miniature blizzard. Leafing through the case histories, one name in particular caught her eye. The diagnosis under Virginia Thornhill's name was a single word spelled *p-r-e-g-n-a-n-t*. So Virginia was sick! No wonder her eyes didn't look right. Amanda wondered what she had. She'd ask Lucille what the word meant. Lucille wouldn't know where she'd seen it. Amanda put the papers back in an upside-down pile and replaced the paperweight.

When Amanda peeked into the examining room, Lucille was putting instruments into a sterilizer.

"What does 'pregnant' mean, Lucille?"

Lucille said nothing for a long time, then, "Where did you see that word?"

Amanda didn't expect that question. She ran the tip of her tongue over the roof of her mouth and felt her temples burn.

Lucille turned to Amanda and glared at her. "Did you look at those case histories?"

Amanda nodded. She stiffened her knees to keep them from buckling. This was trouble. "I didn't think it would matter. I just wondered what Virginia Thornhill had."

"Come here. I want to show you something." Lucille sounded stern.

Amanda's hands shook and her voice rasped. "Are you going to tell Daddy?"

"If I do, I may lose my job, and you'd get the spanking you deserve."

Lucille lose her job? A spanking for looking at a few sheets of paper? Amanda found it hard to believe. After all, she hadn't made a mess. It would be different if she'd spilled ink all over everything.

Lucille led Amanda to her desk and took out a round eraser with a narrow black brush on it. "Do you know what this is?"

"Sure," said Amanda. "It's an eraser. For type-writers."

"That's right." Lucille handed Amanda a pencil. "I want you to print Virginia Thornhill's name on this sheet of paper." Amanda hesitated.

"Go ahead. Print it."

Amanda printed it.

"Now I want you to erase it with this." Lucille handed Amanda the eraser. Amanda erased it because

Mama and Daddy had told her to do exactly what Lucille asked, but she thought it was crazy.

"Now let's take a look at the paper. What do you see?" asked Lucille.

Amanda stared at the sheet. "Eraser crumbs."

"All right," said Lucille. "Brush them into the waste-basket."

Amanda did as she was told.

"Now let's take another look at the paper." Lucille held it up in front of Amanda. "What do you see?"

"A sheet of paper," said Amanda.

Lucille crumpled it and tossed it into the waste-basket. "Amanda, promise me that you will erase from your mind whatever you saw on the patient's records. It's secret information and must not go beyond these walls. Say 'I promise.' Now."

"I promise," said Amanda.

Lucille handed Amanda the eraser. "Keep this as a reminder."

"Gee, thanks." Amanda looked hard at Lucille. "What does 'pregnant' mean?"

"If you saw it on one of the charts, I can't answer." Lucille swallowed and spoke in a hushed tone. "Besides, it's not a nice word."

"Can't I talk about it even to you?" asked Amanda.

Lucille walked into the examining room and turned around. "No." She closed the door, and Amanda watched her blurred shape move behind the frosted glass marked PRIVATE. Amanda stared at the eraser in her hand. Grown-ups! She'd have to keep the secret, but she'd find out what that not-so-nice word meant!

As she came out of Daddy's office onto Main Street, Amanda saw an amazing thing. Parked right there in front of the door was the truck with the license plate 6F–4469. He's in town! Maybe as close as he was last Saturday night! This time she wouldn't hesitate. She'd ask him about Mazda first thing. She'd look in all the stores. She started with the drugstore to the right of Daddy's office and worked her way down to the south end of Main. She didn't see Jack. The only person she recognized was Mr. Schwartz, who was buying a big sack of something at the feed store. She ducked so he wouldn't see her. He gave her the creeps. Then she looked in every store north of Daddy's office. Jack wasn't in any of those either. Then when Amanda went back to check on the truck, it was gone. Gone! It wasn't fair!

On the way home, a cold wind whipped through Amanda's coat. She shivered and put her hands in her pockets. The bristles on the eraser brush poked through her wool mitten as she walked toward the old brick public library. She had an idea. She could look up the word *pregnant* in the library's big dictionary. Besides, it would be warm in there.

Inside, Miss Barney, the librarian, was checking out a book to a man in a long, black overcoat. Amanda looked to see if it was Jack. It wasn't. Amanda moved a chair up to the dictionary stand and stood on it. Just as she opened the heavy book to the *p*'s, Miss Barney spoke.

"May I help you find something, Amanda?"

Amanda closed the dictionary. "No, thank you." She

hopped down and went into the children's stacks. Without bothering to look at the title, she pulled out a book. When she saw Miss Barney disappear into the back office, she went to the big dictionary again. She found the *pr*'s, then the *pre*'s. Her finger moved down the column until she found *pregnant*.

"Why, Amanda!" said a familiar voice. "Imagine finding you here. That dictionary is nearly as big as you are."

Before Amanda could read the definition, she slammed the book shut and turned around.

There stood Mrs. Harpool wiping the frost off her glasses with a flowered handkerchief. "What are you looking up, dear?"

Amanda stared at Mrs. Harpool and said nothing. She knew her face looked as hot as it felt.

Mrs. Harpool gave Amanda a searching look. "Do you want Miss Barney to help you?"

"No. She already offered," whispered Amanda.

"Oh, there's Miss Barney at her desk. I want her to find me some books on Africa. Our missionary society is studying Africa this winter. I hope she has some decent books without all those naked pictures in them." Mrs. Harpool rushed over to Miss Barney.

Amanda picked up the book she'd left on the children's table. Had Mrs. Harpool seen the word she was looking up? Just her luck! Caught by the biggest gossip in town.

Mrs. Harpool was trying to whisper to Miss Barney, but it was hard for Mrs. Harpool to do anything quietly. Amanda heard every word.

"Doris, keep an eye on Amanda Albee over there. When children that age hang around a dictionary, they're usually up to no good. There are plenty of words children have no business seeing."

Amanda pretended to read as she waited for Mrs. Harpool and Miss Barney to disappear, but they were hurrying about gathering books from every corner of the library, in plain sight. Amanda lost hope for another try at the dictionary and left.

Two blocks from home, Amanda stopped in front of the Latimers' house to pet Clancy. He sat on the sidewalk in front of Amanda, shivering and panting white breath clouds. The oatmeal was gone. So was the paper under it.

"Good boy, Clancy. Gee, you didn't have to eat the paper." Amanda gave him a hug. "I can't stay, but I'll bring you some of my dinner."

At home, when Amanda walked into the front room, a wave of disappointment swept over her. Their Christmas tree was an oleander bush Mama kept in the house all winter. Last night, they'd put tinsel and shiny balls on the long, green leaves. Amanda thought it looked awful and was ashamed to have Louise or anyone else see it. Mama said that if they did without a tree, they'd have enough money to fill a basket for the Hinkle family, who lived in a shack down by the river. Whenever Amanda saw that silly little bush trying to look like a Christmas tree, she felt angry — at the Hinkles.

When Amanda was sure that Mama was too busy in the kitchen to notice her, she slipped the dictionary out of the bookshelf and leafed through the *p*'s until she found the word. She read its meaning: "containing unborn young within the body." Then she read it over and over. The only other word Amanda knew that meant about the same thing was *confinement*. Daddy often spoke of "confinements" at the hospital. Her breath came fast, and her heart pounded in her ears. Virginia Thornhill was going to have a baby! And she wasn't married!

Amanda knew about one other unmarried Prairie Bend girl who'd had a baby. It had happened years ago, but people still talked about her as that "unfortunate young woman." Amanda didn't understand why, but she knew Virginia's family would be disgraced, and the baby would go to an orphanage. That other girl went to Kansas City when she started to get fat, and when she came back to Prairie Bend all thin again, some people wouldn't speak to her or have anything to do with her family. So they moved and never set foot in Prairie Bend again. Amanda wondered what the Thornhills would do. Horror and excitement fought inside her. Amanda felt she'd burst if she didn't shout it out right this minute. She wanted to run in and tell Mama, but she couldn't. Mama would tell Daddy, and she'd be in trouble. Margaret might tell Daddy, too. Louise could keep a secret, but . . .

Amanda took the eraser out of her coat pocket, twirled the gray rubber wheel, and stroked the long black bristles. If she told, and Daddy found out, she'd be punished for snooping into his case histories. Then if Lucille was fired for not hiding the records in a better place, it would be Amanda's fault. And she'd promised. She slowly swept the eraser brush across her lips. No wonder Lucille had acted the way she did. The news would rock the town. If the Thornhills moved away before Virginia got fat — Amanda shuddered. Mr. Thornhill could never run for mayor now! She slid the dictionary back into its place. Aside from Virginia, unless she had told her parents, only three people in the whole world knew: Daddy, Lucille, and — herself. She felt as if she'd swallowed a stick of sputtering dynamite that could go off any minute unless she moved carefully — and silently.

Amanda took the eraser to her room. With trembling fingers, she placed it alongside Grandpa's gold piece in the cigar box. She could tell no one. How she wished Mazda were in the back yard right now. She could always talk to Mazda. Until she got him back, she'd tell Clancy all about it. Only one trouble with Clancy. The Latimers often took him inside when she needed him the most.

❦ *Chapter 9* ❦

On Christmas day, Mama, Hal, Margaret, and Amanda were finishing the dishes after dinner.

"What a wonderful Christmas it's been," said Mama.

Amanda looked out the window. "We're having snow." With mixed feelings, she watched big flakes whiten the ground. On any other Christmas, she would have been thrilled to have snow. But today she wouldn't be able to try out her new roller skates. Not until it melted, and that might take several days.

"Just look," said Daddy. "Presents from people all over town." He put his arm around Amanda. The two of them stood there admiring the gifts piled high on the dining room buffet. Hattie had sent popcorn balls for Amanda, Margaret, and Hal. There were decorated cookies from Lucille and hand-embroidered pillowcases from the nuns at the hospital. And Mr. Breen, the druggist, sent over a large box of Whitman's chocolates. The Whitman's chocolates reminded Amanda of Mayor Butler and Mazda. Poor Mazda! Who could guess where he was or how he was being treated on this Christmas day. Every time she went anywhere she looked for Jack. So far, no luck.

On the sideboard with the other gifts, Amanda noticed a book on Africa Mrs. Harpool had given Mama. Mrs. Harpool had explained that it was a decent book with no naked pictures in it. Mrs. Latimer brought fruitcake, and Mrs. Spriggs came over with a plate of fudge. There were a hundred and nine cards from patients and friends. Amanda knew because she'd counted them. And relatives in Colorado wrote saying they were sorry they couldn't be in Prairie Bend for Christmas. Mr. Schwartz had delivered a dressed goose to Daddy's office, most of which they'd eaten for Christmas dinner.

Just before they'd sat down at the table, Mama had said, "Please don't tell Grandpa where the goose came from. If he finds out before dinner, he won't eat a bite, and if he finds out after, he may be pretty unhappy." So no one told Grandpa where the goose came from.

The doorbell rang. When Daddy went to answer it, Amanda sat on the floor and tried on her shiny new skates for the tenth time. She was tightening the toe clamps over her shoes with a key when she looked up. As Daddy held the door open, she saw a man in a long black overcoat standing on the porch. Snowflakes were collecting on the brim of his hat, which was pulled down over one side of his head. His coat collar was turned up, and all Amanda could see of his face was one shadowy eye.

"Are you Dr. Albee?" asked the man in a half-whisper.

"Why, yes," said Daddy. "What can I do for you?"

For a second, Amanda thought the voice sounded

like one she'd heard before, but when he went on in that hushed tone, she changed her mind.

The man handed Daddy a package. "Mayor Butler sent this to you and said to tell you Merry Christmas."

"Thank you," said Daddy. "Won't you come in?"

"No thanks," said the man. "I have some other deliveries to make."

"Well, Merry Christmas," said Daddy. The man hurried off. Daddy looked inside the sack, then he pulled out a large, round bottle of something the color of strong tea. He studied its label.

Mama looked over Daddy's shoulder and gasped. "Why, it's whiskey! From Mayor Butler? Howard! I can't believe my eyes. He must have bought it from a bootlegger!"

Whiskey! From a bootlegger! Amanda felt shocked and excited at the same time.

"Looks like Ol' Man Schwartz's business is growin' like a canker sore," said Grandpa.

"Was that Mr. Schwartz at the door?" asked Margaret.

"Nope," said Grandpa. "Ol' Man Schwartz is too smart to deliver it himself. He'd rather let someone else be caught by the sheriff."

Mama grew pale. "If we keep it here, we could be arrested. You'll have to get rid of it right now, Howard."

Daddy laughed. "Well, Martha, it's asking a lot of me to down it all at once."

Mama drew her lips into a straight line. "Howard! It's no joking matter. We're violating the law this minute!"

Daddy put the bottle back in the sack. "I could flush it down the toilet."

"Howard!" cried Mama.

"It's pretty strong, Daddy," said Hal. "It could ruin the pipes."

"And someone might see the bottle in the trash," said Margaret.

Mama sighed. "Don't you see what having it in the house is doing? The children are talking about it. That should never happen, Howard."

Daddy stared straight ahead. "Well, Martha, it seems that the only thing to do is take it away from here." A slow smile spread across his face. "And I just happened to think of the most secret place in the whole world." He put on his coat and kissed Mama. "And Martha, I can assure you that you will never see this bottle, nor hear about it again."

"May I go with you, Daddy?" asked Amanda. She wanted to know where the most secret place in the whole world was.

"All right, Little Kitten. Bundle up." Daddy twisted the sack around the bottle and tucked it into his deep coat pocket.

"Where are you taking it, Howard?" asked Mama.

Daddy smiled at Mama. "Martha, I think it would be far better for you not to know. Just put it out of your mind, my dear."

"Be careful, Howard," said Mama. "If the sheriff stops you, you'll be in deep trouble."

"Martha," Daddy said, holding Mama by the shoulders and looking into her eyes, "I've been driving cars for many years and I've never been stopped by the sheriff."

In the car, Amanda watched the windshield wipers sweep clear, wet arches on the snowy glass. After a short drive through swirling whiteness, Daddy stopped the car in front of the hospital.

"Are you taking the whiskey to the hospital, Daddy?" asked Amanda.

"Can you keep a secret, Little Kitten?"

Amanda knew she was keeping more secrets now than she could handle. There was that big one stalking her like a tiger just waiting to tear her to pieces — the pregnant Virginia Thornhill. And all those other secrets: her search for Mazda, and those scary, dizzy feelings about Jack. And today Mama wouldn't let her tell Grandpa where the goose came from. She didn't really want another secret. But, on the other hand, she just had to know where Daddy was taking the whiskey.

Daddy smiled at her. "Well?"

Big flakes covered the car windows. It was as if the two of them were sitting there in an igloo, shut away from the rest of the world.

Amanda heaved a sigh and said, "Yes, Daddy."

"All right, then. Come along." When they got out and shut the car doors, snow slid off the windows into the sparkling blanket below.

Whenever Amanda passed through those big, double hospital doors, it was like being plunked down on a different planet, a shiny clean world, hushed, and smelling of ether. In the hall stood a statue of the Virgin Mary even bigger than Daddy, draped in robes painted blue and pink and gold, and holding out waxy hands. At the very end of the hall was a statue of Jesus on the cross. He was a gray color with death in every shadow of His face and body. Amanda tried not to look.

A nun in a long, black robe glided toward them. A loop of beads with a gold cross on it swung from some secret fold in her skirts.

"Sister Theresa," said Daddy, "Merry Christmas to you."

"Merry Christmas and God bless you, Dr. Albee," replied Sister Theresa. "I see you brought your helper with you this evening."

"Sister, this is my daughter Amanda. I wonder if we might have a few words with the mother superior."

"She's just finishing prayers, doctor. I'll tell her you're here." Sister Theresa disappeared through a frosted glass door near the statue of Jesus.

When the mother superior came, she held out her hand to Daddy. Though her cheeks and forehead were nearly hidden by what looked like white cardboard hung with black cloth, Amanda could see that she was fatter and jollier looking than Sister Theresa. She smiled as she looked down at Amanda.

"Mother Mary Joseph, this is my daughter Amanda," said Daddy. "We came to wish you a merry Christmas, and hope that you will find a place for this." Daddy handed her the sack with the bottle in it.

Mother Mary Joseph peeked inside the paper bag and, in the same level voice she might use in a sickroom, said, "Yes, Doctor. Good medicine is always welcome." Then she lifted a corner of her black skirt and tucked the sack completely out of sight. It was all done so quickly that Amanda thought it seemed like a magician's trick.

"God bless you, doctor," said the mother superior. "And you, my dear." She placed her hand on Amanda's head.

As they drove home through the snowy streets, Amanda asked, "Daddy, do nuns drink whiskey?"

"No one knows for sure, Amanda," said Daddy. "But don't forget, my dear, that whiskey is often used for medicinal purposes."

"Daddy, wouldn't it be a sin if the sisters drank it?"

"Yes, Little Kitten," he said, "but they sin so little that it would probably average out pretty well."

Amanda said nothing, but she felt that sinning would be worse if the mother superior did it.

Later, Amanda walked the two blocks through the snow to Clancy's. As she fed him a piece of meat from Mr. Schwartz's goose, she heard a car coming down the street and looked up. It wasn't a car. It was a truck. When it went by, Amanda noticed that the driver had his coat collar turned up around his face and a hat pulled over one eye. When the truck passed her, Amanda read the license number. 6F–4469. She stood there, stunned, watching the truck grow smaller and smaller until it turned a distant corner.

Amanda knelt down in the snow and spoke to Clancy in a quaking voice. "Clancy, do you know who that was?" Clancy licked her fingers. "Would you believe it? Jack! He's been delivering whiskey! And, Clancy, there's something else you'd never believe."

The dog licked Amanda's cheek.

"Clancy, do you know what the most secret place in the whole world is?"

He looked up at Amanda with his soft brown eyes.

Amanda whispered in his ear, "The pocket of a nun's petticoat."

❧ *Chapter 10* ❧

*T*he late March sunshine warmed Amanda's head as she skated home with Louise.

Amanda shouted above the *shush-shush* of steel rollers on the sidewalk. "After we go home, let's skate around the courthouse." The courthouse walks slanted down to the street, great for coasting. Amanda went there a lot and watched for Jack or his truck.

"I can't go to the courthouse today," yelled Louise.

Amanda had seen Jack three times since Christmas. Once, just driving by, and once coming out of the Wild Goose Cafe. That time, he drove off before she could get there. Another time, she saw his back disappear into the Strand Theatre, and she had no dime for a ticket. But she was still determined to find Mazda.

"Hey!" Louise pointed straight ahead. "Let's catch up with Billy!"

"Sure," cried Amanda. "Then we can play with Dandy." They slowed down just behind Billy Thornhill, Virginia's kid brother. His shaggy black dog, Dandy, heeled along at his side. Amanda loved the way Dandy always met Billy at the same corner after school. Whenever Amanda saw Billy, her thoughts turned to the eraser in her cigar box. It was spring already. Why hadn't the Thornhills moved? Amanda had seen Virginia several times. She was getting fat right here in Prairie Bend, and people were talking.

"Hi, Billy," said Amanda. He just walked on without a word.

"What's the matter?" asked Louise. Amanda had often heard Miss Forbes ask Billy that same question; he didn't seem to talk much now. Amanda knew why.

Just as Amanda and Louise stopped to pet Dandy, three older boys crossed the street and ran toward them.

One in a striped shirt shouted, "Hey, Bill! When did your sister swallow the watermelon seed?" The others giggled.

Dandy barked at the boys. Billy's face reddened, and tears filled his eyes. Then he turned and walked away as fast as he could.

Amanda skated in front of the big boys and said, "Leave him alone!"

"Hee, hee, hee!" a red-haired one snickered. "You're just a little kid. I'll bet you don't know what we was laughin' about."

It was all Amanda could do to keep from saying, "I do too!" She bit her lip and kept her mind on the eraser. "Pick on somebody your own size," she yelled.

The boy in the striped shirt spat on the sidewalk. "Just look who's talkin'! Pip Squeak here thinks she can order the big guys around. C'mon fellas! Let's catch up with him!"

Dandy barked when he saw them coming, and Billy

put his hands over his ears. The three boys followed Billy and his dog around the corner and out of sight.

"What was that all about?" asked Louise.

"Who knows?" said Amanda. It was a trick answer. The gossip about Virginia tugged at her guilt feelings. She could kick herself for looking at those secret records. But she had never said a word. She was sure Lucille and Daddy had never said anything either.

The afternoon was growing really warm when Amanda took off her skates on the back porch. Through the open door, she saw Mama beating egg whites. It was Margaret's birthday. She'd almost forgotten. And Mama was making a cake.

"Is it angel food?" asked Amanda.

Mama smiled. "Yes, and I want you to go to Reuter's store to get birthday candles."

"Sure." Amanda was glad for an excuse to go downtown to look for Jack. "Where is Margaret?"

"In our bedroom."

"Is she reading that book?"

"Yes," said Mama. "It's her birthday."

"Shucks. Now I'll be the only one who doesn't know everything. It's not fair."

Mama laughed. "No one knows everything, dear. Just remember, you'll get to read it in another year and a half." Mama opened her purse and handed Amanda a fifty cent piece. "Here, Amanda. Buy cake candles and two sixty-watt light bulbs."

Light bulbs, thought Amanda, with "Mazda" printed

on each one. Mazda! How she'd love to feed him, hold him, and stroke him again! And she had so much to tell him! She had to find Jack!

On her way downtown, Amanda stopped by the Latimers' to see if Clancy was out. He wasn't. Darn! The spring sunshine felt hot. She sat on a curb, rolled her tan ribbed stockings to her ankles, and pushed her long white underwear above her knees. The fresh breeze felt good on her bare legs.

Inside the store, Amanda saw Mrs. Latimer studying a list.

"Let me see," she said, "I'll have a half-dozen bananas." Mr. Reuter pulled six bananas off the stalk that hung from the ceiling and put them in a sack. Then Mrs. Latimer saw Amanda.

"Oh, hello, Amanda," she said. "I've been meaning to talk to you about something."

Amanda suspected the "something" had to do with Clancy. Her hands went cold, and her knees shook.

"I know you love Clancy, dear," said Mrs. Latimer, "but the food you leave on our sidewalk has become a messy problem. Pet him all you like, Amanda, but please don't bring him any more food." She turned to Mr. Reuter and said, "How much do I owe you?"

Mrs. Latimer's words lashed out at Amanda like cruel blows. A pet you couldn't feed was no pet at all. She had to get Mazda back. An aching lump swelled in her throat, and to keep the tears from spilling down, she tried not to blink. She wouldn't cry. She wouldn't! Amanda moved away from Mrs. Latimer and stood by two other ladies near the meat counter. Amanda had seen them before, but didn't know their names.

The first one said, "You'd think Walter Thornhill would have sense enough to send her away."

The other one said, "My husband saw her walking down Main Street last week. Can you imagine? Main Street! In such a condition. He tried to get a good look, but she was carrying a big sheet of cardboard in front of her. When he asked what she was going to do with it, she said, 'I'm making a poster for school.' A poster! Hah!" Amanda tried to think about the eraser, but she couldn't. Mrs. Latimer's words still stung.

Then the first woman said, "I hear it's due in June. It's tragic. It's just tragic. And her sister Dorothy so talented and all. She's just ruining her whole family. She's a bad girl. There's no doubt about it. I feel so sorry for her parents. Mabel, you and I don't know how lucky we are to have good daughters."

Amanda inched closer to the ladies. Tragic? Why? Amanda wondered. A bad girl? Why? Ruining her whole family? Why? Why was it so terrible to have a baby when you weren't married? Why? Why? Why? Amanda's urge to ask the ladies all those whys was so strong she had to stop it. She thought of the eraser and said nothing.

The lady named Mabel looked at Amanda and then she said to the other one, "Little pitchers have big ears. We'd better talk somewhere else."

The other one whispered, "That's Dr. Albee's daughter. She probably knows all about it."

Amanda bit her lips and turned away. She thought so hard about the eraser, she could feel its gritty wheel and stiff bristles. She kept her mind on it until the ladies left.

Mr. Reuter looked down at Amanda and said, "What can I do for you today, young lady?"

Amanda smiled. "I want a box of cake candles and two sixty-watt erasers." When she saw Mr. Reuter's puzzled look, she finally heard her own words hanging in the air and throbbing in the silence. A burning flush grew from the roots of her hair to fiery waves on her forehead. "I meant sixty-watt light bulbs." She hung her head.

When Amanda left the store, she glanced up and down Main Street for Jack. When she didn't see him, she looked for the truck. The truck wasn't on the store side of Main Street, so she crossed over to the court-house side. Before she got all the way across, she saw it. It was parked third from the corner. To Amanda, the license number stood out like a movie marquee. She quivered all over. How long would she have to wait? She didn't dare run home with the bulbs and candles. Sure as anything, the truck would be gone when she got back. She'd have to wait no matter what Mama said.

She sat on the curb between the truck and the car parked next to it, and let the hot sun warm her hair and shoulders. Minutes passed. She got up and walked around the truck. In back there was a gunnysack of chicken feed and flour in a big cotton bag with blossoms printed on it — the kind of cloth farmers' wives and poor people made into dresses. Then she sat down on the curb in front of the driver's side of the truck and opened the sack from Reuter's. She was counting the birthday candles when, right behind her, she heard a voice she recognized.

"Git outa my way. You're blockin' traffic."

Amanda jumped and spun around. It was Mr. Schwartz.

"Why don't you shut yer mouth? You look like a fish outa water."

Amanda stared at him in disbelief. Then anger swallowed her fear. She stomped her foot and yelled, "I'm not a fish, and I have as much right to be here as you do!"

Mr. Schwartz's black eyes glittered as he looked into her face. "I'd like to wring that sassy little neck o' yours."

Amanda shuddered. She watched him climb into the truck and slam the door. Mr. Schwartz and Jack drove the same truck! So Jack worked for Mr. Schwartz! It didn't surprise her, since Jack had delivered the whiskey. She was afraid to say another word to him, but she had to. She took a deep breath and blurted out, "Where's Jack?"

Mr. Schwartz leaned out the window. "Heh, heh, heh!" Even his laugh sounded mean. "Ain't you a little young to be chasin' after him? Hear he's quite the lady killer. Must have all ages moonin' after him."

Amanda's face burned, mostly from anger. "I'm not chasing after anybody!" she shouted. "He's got my rooster, and I want him back!"

Mr. Schwartz started the truck. "Forgit it. You're

talkin' about the best fightin' cock in seven counties. After your daddy operated and took all my money, I'm glad to have that Albee bird fillin' my pockets. Mighty glad." His grin showed his missing teeth.

Amanda stared at him. How dare he say Daddy "took" his money like some thief! And Mazda! Risking his life! To make gambling money for Mr. Schwartz! Rage boiled up inside her and exploded. "Don't talk about my daddy like that!" she screamed. "And Jack stole my rooster! He's mine!"

"Heh, heh, heh! Whatta ya know! Looks like I'm gettin' even with the stuck-up Albees! 'Course, when your rooster's fightin' days are over, I could bring him to your daddy all cooked up in a Mason jar. Oughta be worth fifty cents on my bill."

Amanda gasped. Every muscle in her body shook.

Mr. Schwartz scowled. "But you'll have to wait a while. He's still a winner. And then my missus ain't done much cannin' since she started bellyachin'." He stepped on the gas and screeched his tires on the hot pavement. In a second, he was gone.

Amanda stood there at the empty parking space until she stopped shaking so much and then she started home. Who could have guessed Mazda would end up with the meanest man in the whole world? How could Jack stand to work for him? The words "all cooked up in a Mason jar" haunted her. So did "He's still a winner." How long would he win? He could end up lame — or dead! Poor Mazda! No telling what he'd been through. And she'd promised Grandma she'd take good care of him. Grandma hated gambling and would be shocked to know that her gift was being used in such a terrible way.

Amanda had to rescue him. No question about it. But how? She didn't even know where Mr. Schwartz lived. If his farm was only a mile or two from town, she could walk there. But if it was a long way, then what?

At home, when Amanda set the candles and light bulbs on the kitchen table, she smelled the cake baking and she heard Mama talking on the phone.

"Oh, Tess!" cried Mama. "You must be mistaken. I can't believe it. Not Virginia Thornhill!" Amanda wondered if anyone in town was talking about anything else. She didn't stay to listen. She was thinking about something more important. She had to find out where Mr. Schwartz lived. Grandpa might know.

Amanda found Grandpa sitting on the porch swing, reading the newspaper, and sat down beside him. "Grandpa, where does Mr. Schwartz live?"

"Ten miles east on Ninety-four."

"Highway Ninety-four?"

"That's right. Why?"

"Just wondered," said Amanda. Ten miles! Twenty both ways. It would take days to walk that far, and Mama and Daddy would never let her. She'd have to get a ride, but who would be going there? Only one person she knew. Virginia Thornhill. That is, if she and Jack were still seeing each other. Amanda hopped down from the swing. The thought of Mazda on that horrible man's farm gave her all the courage she needed. She peeked into the house and saw Mama still talking on the phone. She ran around back and kept on going for four blocks until she came to the Thornhills' yellow house with the curved front porch.

After all that gossip about Virginia, Amanda felt that running up the Thornhill's front steps was a forbidden thing to do, like entering a house with a scarlet fever or smallpox sign in the window — a diseased and quarantined house. The Thornhills' car, a new Hudson, was parked out front. Quarantined or not, thought Amanda, it would be fun to ride in such a fancy car. But her thoughts were silly, she told herself. Babies weren't catching like smallpox or scarlet fever. Or were they? As she twisted the doorbell, Amanda heard Dorothy practicing her violin. Then the playing stopped and the door opened. Dorothy held her violin and bow in one hand and the door with the other.

"Is Virginia home?" Amanda's voice sounded strange even to her own ears, several notes higher than normal.

"Why?" asked Dorothy.

"I want to ask her something."

"She's not seeing anyone right now," said Dorothy. "She's resting." Amanda was sorry she'd come.

"Who is it?" asked a voice behind Dorothy.

"Amanda Albee says she wants to ask you something."

"I'll talk to her." Virginia came to the door. The loose fitting gown she wore couldn't hide her swollen stomach. To keep from staring, Amanda looked down at her shoes and thought about the eraser.

"What is it, Amanda? Your rooster?" Virginia's voice was soft and kind.

Amanda looked up and nodded. "My rooster is at the Schwartzes' farm, and I want him back. If you go there sometime, will you take me?"

"Take you?" Virginia's eyebrows arched as if she didn't understand.

Amanda took a deep breath and tried again. "When you drive out there in your father's eraser, would you take me?"

"My father's what?" Virginia's eyes widened.

Amanda couldn't believe she'd said those silly words. Her face burned. She shouldn't have come. "I — um — meant Hudson."

Virginia came out on the porch and closed the door behind her. "Amanda, I don't even want to talk about the Schwartzes' farm. No. I wouldn't think of taking you there. It's too bad about your rooster."

"Maybe you could bring him to me, then," said Amanda. "He's orange and yellow and brown. And he has green and black tail feathers and three tiny white dots on his comb. My grandma gave him to me when he was a tiny chick, and —"

Virginia interrupted her. "Amanda, I know how badly you must feel, but you're asking the impossible."

"Why?"

"Well, for one thing, I just can't go and take things away from Mr. Schwartz." She sighed.

Amanda understood. She looked down at her shoes again.

"I'm sorry," said Virginia. "But there's really nothing I can do."

On the way home, Amanda kicked at rocks and

sticks. Not only did she have to find another way to get to the Schwartzes' farm, but she was sick to death of thinking about that eraser. Two slips of the tongue in one day! How embarrassing! She'd ask Daddy some questions at supper — careful questions. Maybe — just maybe she wouldn't have to keep that secret anymore. After all, what did it matter that she saw Virginia's chart? Everybody in town was talking about her anyway.

At supper, Amanda stared at Margaret. She looked the same. Somehow Amanda expected her to look different after reading that book.

After Margaret blew out her birthday candles, Hal asked, "What did you wish?"

"If I tell, it won't come true," said Margaret.

"Aw," Hal scoffed, "that's just an old wives' tale."

"Any old wife I ever knew would have better sense than to believe such superstitious rubbish," said Grandpa.

Before Grandpa could get started on superstition, Amanda decided to ask Daddy the first question.

"Daddy, what if somebody saw one of your patient's charts? Would it be wrong for that person to talk about it?"

Daddy gave Amanda a searching look. "Why in the world are you asking that question?"

Amanda shrugged. "I just wondered." Amanda amazed herself. She was acting so cool and calm. But her head throbbed and her stomach churned. Something in Daddy's face frightened her. The vein. The vein on his forehead stood out. Did he suspect?

Daddy frowned as he looked into her eyes. "Well, it

most certainly would be wrong, Amanda. Those records are confidential. Strictly secret. Thank goodness I have an office girl I can trust. Lucille would never let anyone see my case histories, and she'd never say a word about them." Daddy looked down at his plate and started to eat.

Amanda couldn't catch her breath. When she tried, the air wouldn't go down. She stared dizzily at the angel cake in front of her.

"Amanda, are you all right?" asked Mama. "You look pale."

Amanda's voice came in a whisper. "I'm fine." She studied Daddy's face. It looked unusually stern. If she slipped out of this tight spot without being punished, she knew she'd never be able to forget the eraser.

Suddenly, Daddy changed the subject. "Well, Father, what did you do today?"

Amanda took a deep breath, all the way to the bottom of her lungs.

"Listened to a trial down at the courthouse." Grandpa took the thick piece of cake Mama handed him.

"Sounds interesting," said Daddy. "Who's suing whom these days?"

"*Bestwick versus Schwartz,*" said Grandpa. "Seems that Lester Schwartz has been grazin' his cattle on Frank Bestwick's wheat. Schwartz denies it o' course, but Bestwick's got a smart young lawyer. I'll bet ten to one Schwartz has to pay damages."

"Hmmm!" said Daddy. "The Bestwicks are patients of mine."

Amanda started to listen with a rush of interest. "Do the Bestwicks live near the Schwartzes?"

"Yep," said Grandpa, "right next door. Some people have cyclones and floods and rattlesnakes, but the Bestwicks have Ol' Man Schwartz. He's worse'n all three."

Amanda was so excited she could hardly sit still. Daddy had patients living next door to the Schwartzes! She wondered what next door meant in the country. A mile? She could walk a mile.

"Daddy," she said, "do you ever call on the Bestwicks?"

"From time to time, Little Kitten. Why?"

"Do they have dogs and cats and cows and horses?" she asked.

"They have several of each," said Grandpa. "It came out in the trial."

"Will you take me along the next time you go to the Bestwicks', Daddy? To see their animals?"

Daddy smiled. "I'd be happy to arrange that, Amanda. Those long rides in the country get to be pretty lonely sometimes."

Things were looking a little better for Mazda's rescue, but there were some big *ifs*. Amanda weighed her chances. If Daddy was ever called to the Bestwicks', and if it wasn't during school hours, she might be able to go along and walk from there to the Schwartzes'. But the Bestwicks might never call Daddy. And if one of them did get sick, they could just drive into town to see him. She knew she was spinning a weak thread of hope, but it was better than nothing.

Grandpa examined the white fluff on the end of his fork. "Does this cake have Ol' Man Schwartz's eggs in it?"

"I bought the eggs at the store, Grandpa," said Mama. "I didn't ask Mr. Reuter where they came from."

"That's the trouble nowadays," said Grandpa. "The good and the bad get all scrambled up. You could be swallerin' evil food all the time and never know it."

Amanda watched Mama and Daddy glance at each other and smile just the way they always did when they thought she was being funny and ridiculous.

That night, as they lay in bed, Amanda snuggled close to Margaret and whispered, "What was in the book? Tell me."

"I can't. I promised I wouldn't," said Margaret.

Amanda tried again. "Margaret, do you know why it's so terrible to have a baby when you're not married?"

Margaret sighed and said, "Go to sleep, Amanda."

After a while, Margaret whispered, "Amanda, are you still awake?"

Amanda rolled over on her back. "Uh-huh."

Margaret cupped her hand around Amanda's ear and whispered, "Have you heard about Virginia Thornhill?"

Amanda's heart raced. They might make a deal! Tell each other their secrets! Could she talk about Virginia and not mention the records? She wanted to more than anything. It was dangerous, though. One slip and she'd be in trouble. Then there was the eraser right here in this room, no more than a few feet away, lying there in the cigar box. And she'd promised Lucille.

Amanda turned over. "Go to sleep, Margaret."

Long after Margaret's breathing had dropped into snoozing rhythm, Amanda lay awake and listened to Mama and Daddy talking in their bedroom.

"Howard, I heard the most incredible thing today. Tess Harpool told me that Virginia Thornhill is expecting a baby. Do you know anything about it?"

"Virginia Thornhill?" Daddy's voice sounded sleepy.

"Yes. Virginia Thornhill."

"Walter Thornhill's daughter?" he asked.

"Yes. Walter's daughter."

Daddy paused and then said, "Hmmmmmm!"

Mama sighed. "Well, Howard, obviously it's news to you. I'm so relieved."

Amanda's body stiffened. She pulled the covers up over her mouth. Daddy couldn't tell Mama the truth even when she asked for it.

When the house grew quiet, Amanda fell into a restless sleep. She dreamed that she fed Clancy, and Mrs. Latimer chased her away with a butcher knife. Then she dreamed that Daddy spanked her and fired Lucille, and that Lucille was so mad at her she chased her around the block with Mrs. Latimer's butcher knife. When she caught Amanda, the knife was gone, but Lucille shook her and screamed at her to give the eraser back. When Amanda looked in the cigar box, it was gone. Lucille had the knife again and was about to stab her, when Daddy floated in from somewhere. He took the knife away from Lucille and gave it to Mama, who suddenly appeared. Then Daddy reached into his vest and pulled something out of his pocket; not the watch he always kept there. She could see it more clearly now. A strange object dangled from his shiny gold chain. It was the eraser. He looked at it as if it were a watch and told her it was time for them to go to the Schwartzes' farm. Then Daddy disappeared, and Mr. Schwartz stepped out of a smoke tunnel. He was holding Mazda by the neck. Poor Mazda was squawking and flapping his wings.

"I'm coming, Mazda!" cried Amanda. "I'm coming!"

In the weeks that followed, Amanda and Louise spent a lot of time skating on the courthouse grounds and watching. Amanda hoped Mr. Schwartz would bring Mazda to town in his truck. Why he would do such a thing, she couldn't imagine, but if he ever did, she'd waste no time grabbing Mazda and running. Twice they saw his truck parked outside the courthouse. Quick searches told them that Mr. Schwartz had not brought Mazda to town.

One Saturday in April, Amanda followed Jack into the pool hall to ask about Mazda. Mama would have killed her for going in there; according to Mama, the pool hall wasn't a respectable place. All Jack said was, "Beat it, kid. Scram!" She would have hidden in the back of his truck, but there was nothing in it to hide behind. Then, late one afternoon in May, she saw him coming out of Buehler's Feed Store, but he drove off before she could catch up with him. In desperation one morning, after school was out for the summer, she and Louise started walking straight east on Ninety-four. They hoped that someone they knew would come along in a car and take them the rest of the way to the Schwartzes' farm, but no one did. After an hour's walk in the heat and dust, they came back.

"I don't think you'll ever get him back," said Louise.

"I will too!" Amanda kicked at pebbles in the road. She hated Louise's words because they spoke the fear that was growing inside her. That night, Amanda added new phrases to her nightly prayer.

"Please, God!" she said. "Let me find Mazda and let him be alive!"

❦ *Chapter 11* ❦

*A*manda sat on the front seat beside Daddy and watched the car's shadow bounce ahead of them like a galloping black ghost. This afternoon, the call came for Daddy to go to the Bestwicks', and here she was. She had waited a long time for this chance. It was summer now. June. The late afternoon heat wrapped around her like a steamy blanket. At last she was on her way to rescue Mazda!

Daddy reached over and tousled her hair. "Glad you could come along, Little Kitten."

Amanda smiled up at Daddy. Guilt nibbled at her conscience. Daddy knew nothing about her secret plan. She'd thought it all out, had seen to every detail. When Daddy went into the Bestwicks' house, she'd ask to stay outside with the dogs or cats or whatever they had. Then she'd dash to the Schwartzes' farm, catch Mazda, bring him back to the car, and put him in one of the gunnysacks Daddy carried in back. There were two. She'd checked. Her plan was simple and shouldn't take more than a few minutes.

"How much farther, Daddy?" Amanda was surprised that her throat felt so dry and her voice sounded squeaky.

"About five more miles. We'll be there shortly."

Shortly! An empty feeling swept through Amanda from her chest to her knees, and her fingers turned to ice. But there was no reason to be nervous. She'd planned everything. While she was at the Schwartzes', she'd crouch down behind bushes and trees. She'd even thought to wear her brown dress instead of the red one so she could hide better.

Neither spoke as they drove on. To take her mind off her errand, Amanda watched for horses and cows along the way. She'd counted twenty-three cows and five horses, when Daddy turned the car into a long, dirt driveway.

"Here we are," he said.

Two yapping dogs met the car and chased it until Daddy parked under a tree near the house.

The time had come! Amanda had to move fast. Daddy got out and reached for his bag. "Want to come in?"

Amanda made herself smile in a way she hoped looked natural. "I'd rather stay out here and play with the dogs, Daddy." That squeaky voice!

Daddy didn't seem to notice. "All right. I won't be long."

Won't be long! She hoped it would be long enough. Daddy walked up the steps of the sagging front porch. A man in overalls opened the door for him. Amanda climbed out of the car and patted the dogs. The black one licked Amanda's cheek. The brown and white one poked his nose at her shoes. They crowded her so with their nuzzling and sniffing that it was hard to move.

What if they followed her to Schwartzes' farm and made a racket? She couldn't let them. She raised all the car windows high enough to keep a dog from jumping out, but low enough to let in plenty of air. She swung the back door of the car wide open and coaxed them inside. When she shut the door, they barked.

"Shhh!" Amanda reached in to pet them. "Now be quiet. I'll let you out soon." The spotted one lay down on the floor panting, and the black one stuck his head out the window.

Amanda ran down the long driveway and out onto the road. Grandpa said the Schwartzes lived due east of the Bestwicks. So, with the sun warming her back, she looked across a yellow wheat field. Barely visible in the distance, a peaked barn top rose above a cluster of trees. That must be it. But it was so far! A mile? Maybe more. She had to run.

Panting, she neared the farm site. She couldn't just walk up the Schwartzes' driveway. She'd be seen. She'd have to sneak into the yard from the side or back. As she came closer, she saw a stretch of pasture next to the trees. Clumps of grass stuck up here and there. She ran across the ditch and spread the fence wires, put one leg through, then the other. Her feet sank into soft, sandy dirt, and grasshoppers bumped against her legs.

After crawling through a second fence, she crept toward the farm yard, hiding herself behind bushes, piles of rotting lumber, and rusty farm tools. So far so good. Nobody around. At last she saw the house. It was a one-story frame cottage needing paint. A long porch stretched across one side. In the driveway stood the

Thornhills' car. Anyway, it looked like the Thornhills' Hudson. Virginia must be here! Amanda crouched behind an old plow, flaky with rust, and watched the chickens. White, brown, and gray ones walked about the yard, but Mazda was nowhere to be seen. What if he wasn't here? But then she hadn't really looked yet. She'd have to cross the driveway and go all around the house and barn.

Voices came from the open doors and windows of the house, softly at first, then louder. But Amanda couldn't make out what they were saying or whose they were. One was a man's and the other a woman's.

She hoped Mr. Schwartz was gone. The screen door opened, and Virginia came out of the house and sat on the steps. She was crying. Her stomach was fatter than ever. Then Jack came out and stood against one of the porch pillars. He lit a cigarette and looked down at Virginia.

"Why won't you?" he said. "We could go downtown and get a license in a few minutes."

Virginia shook her head. Jack sat down beside her and took her hand.

"Look, Ginny. We wouldn't have to live here. We could catch the next train to Texas."

"A freight train?" She sighed. "You seem to forget I'm past due."

Past due! What did that mean? Amanda wondered. Listening to such a private conversation was like watching a play, only here, the porch was the stage — and Amanda knew the players. She couldn't cross the driveway to look for Mazda with Jack and Virginia sitting there. She hoped they'd leave soon. And what about Daddy? What if he was nearly through at the Bestwicks'?

Jack leaned over and kissed Virginia. Amanda's toes tingled as she watched.

"Look," said Jack, "I'll stay until the baby comes, and the three of us can go away together."

Virginia stood up and put her hands on Jack's shoulders. "No, Jack. It won't work." Then she turned away from him and, crying, ran to the car. Jack followed her.

"Ginny! Listen to me!" he cried. The car started and zoomed off in a cloud of dust.

Amanda thought Virginia should have listened to him. If she was Virginia, she would have run away with him in a minute.

Jack stood in the driveway. Then he tossed his cigarette down and ground it out with his heel. He walked on toward the road and out of sight.

Amanda dashed across the driveway and ran to the back of the house, her eyes searching every shadow for green tail feathers. She found the chicken coop, but Mazda wasn't in there. She went around to the far side of the house, and under a window she saw something that made her stop. Lying inside an old tire, she saw a lumpy gunnysack. She inched closer. She didn't like being so near an open window. The sack had SUNSHINE FEEDS stamped on it. Sunshine Feeds! Could it be . . . ? Did she dare hope? She touched it. It moved! Then she heard a familiar sound.

"BUCK, BUCK, BUCK!"

Amanda wanted to shout and scream, Mazda! Mazda!

But she had to be quiet. She untied the sack and reached in. Feathers! Long tail feathers! Her heart raced as she lifted him out. It was Mazda all right! She held him in her arms and ran her fingers over the three little white dots on his comb. He looked the same except that one of his wings drooped. Was it broken?

"What have they done to you?" she whispered. Why was he bundled up? Was someone going to take him somewhere? To a cock fight? Amanda shuddered. With those two fences to climb, Amanda decided it would be easier to carry Mazda in his sack. She was just putting him back in the bag when she heard someone talking to her from the window. It was a woman's voice, weak and whispery.

"Do you live around here?" the voice asked.

Amanda looked up and saw a large woman standing behind the screen. She looked like a ghost. Her chalky face matched the white nightgown she wore. She staggered and fell to her knees. Her gray-circled eyes pleaded with Amanda as she spoke. "Please," she whispered, "tell someone to call a doctor. My stomach's acting up again. It does that once in a while." She placed her hand over her side. "Right here. Feels like a knife in there. We have no phone."

Amanda drew in a sharp breath. She felt surprised that the lady paid no attention to Mazda under her arm. This must be Mr. Schwartz's sick wife! The one Daddy couldn't see unless someone called. She looked horribly ill. Lucky Daddy was nearby.

"My daddy's Dr. Albee, and he's at the Bestwicks'. I'll tell him to come over here right away."

"I'll be waiting." The woman spoke in jerky gasps. "If I — if I live that long."

Hurry! Amanda said to herself. Hurry! With Mazda under her arm, she ran as fast as she could. The poor woman was so sick she could hardly walk or talk. Daddy had to get there in time to save her! Amanda was so worried about Mrs. Schwartz and so excited about finding Mazda, that she dashed across the driveway without looking first. She was all the way across before she realized that a truck was now parked under a tree! It hadn't been there before. And behind it, stood a car! Amanda's scalp tingled as she heard a door open and then slam shut. Was it the truck? Heavy footsteps crunched the gravel and then sped up behind her. She didn't have the nerve to look back. If she saw Mr. Schwartz coming after her, she'd freeze. Holding onto Mazda with a tightened grip, she ran faster and faster. She had to get through those fences before he caught up with her. Her breath came in gasps as she passed a blur of bushes and rusty farm tools. She heard him coming. Closer and closer now! It was good she'd put Mazda back in the bag, she thought. She set him down to spread the fence wires. She'd just climbed through and was reaching down to pick him up, when one hairy hand snatched the gunnysack away, and another grabbed her wrist.

"Where do you think you're goin' with my rooster?" It was Mr. Schwartz's voice! She looked up. Those glaring black eyes! The worst was happening, and she had to live through it somehow. His nose hairs quivered as he tightened his grip.

"What's the matter? Cat bite yer tongue?"

Amanda's stomach whirled and her feet went numb. Her voice shrank to a whisper. "That's my rooster. My grandma gave him to me."

Just then, a fat, bald-headed man came up behind Mr. Schwartz. He was chewing on a short, unlit cigar. Mr. Schwartz handed Mazda to him.

"Hold this, Joe," said Mr. Schwartz. "I got some business to attend to here. This little scamp's been askin' for it." He leaned over the fence and grabbed both Amanda's arms above the elbows, and squeezed them until they hurt. "Now whatcha gonna do?"

Before she could say anything, Joe asked, "What's goin' on here, Schwartz?" He swung the bagged Mazda over his shoulder.

"Jes' keep yer mouth shut and watch how you handle my rooster," said Mr. Schwartz.

"Your rooster?" Joe held out the lumpy sack and stared at it.

"Got a busted wing, but I figger he has a fight or two left in him." Mr. Schwartz lifted Amanda over to his side of the fence. Then he shook her. His blue striped overalls seemed to swim into the black specks and blotches that grew before Amanda's eyes. She couldn't faint. She wouldn't! She'd heard Daddy say that deep breaths sometimes keep you from fainting. She inhaled from the bottom of her lungs. It worked. The black spots thinned, and the blue stripes brightened.

Joe spoke again. "Whatcha gonna do with her, Schwartz?" He put Mazda down on the grass.

"None o' yer business."

"You bet it's my business." Joe worked his stubby cigar over to the other side of his mouth. "Ya gotta stay clean, Schwartz, or it's no deal. Boss's orders. Whose kid is this?"

"Doc Albee's over in Prairie Bend. The little thief! Tryin' to make off with my fightin' cock!" He shook her again. "Mouthy, too. Got enough sass for three kids her size. Her Daddy's got a good racket. Cuts ya open and takes out sompin' ya never heard of, then he's got ya payin' him the rest o' yer life."

"Let her go." The other man shifted his cigar again.

"Whatsa matter? Gotta yella streak?" Mr. Schwartz's upper lip curled. "A lock-up in the storm cellar's what she needs. Teach her a good lesson."

A lock-up! In a storm cellar! She could waste away in there until she died of thirst and starvation! A whirling dizziness spun through her head, and her sight went blotchy again. She fought to breathe deeply.

Joe, who was bigger than Mr. Schwartz, grabbed him by his overall bib, twisted it, and said, "Schwartz, you got chicken feed where your brains oughta be. Kidnapin's out. You hear? Out! Especially some doctor's kid. In a few hours the sheriff's men'd be swarmin' over this place like army ants. And we'd be shut down all over the state. Let her go. Now! Or the deal's off."

Amanda could make little sense out of what Joe said, but she guessed he was talking about the bootlegging business. She felt Mr. Schwartz's grip on her arms relax. Then he turned his back on her. She couldn't believe it! She was free! Free! **FREE!** She scrambled through the fence again. When she reached the second fence, the blotches faded into tiny dots, and by the time she dashed across the ditch to the road, she was seeing clearly. It seemed she was waking from a nightmare except that her arms stung where Mr. Schwartz had held her. Thanks to the man named Joe, she'd gotten away, but she'd had to leave Mazda behind! Poor Mazda! He was hurt. His wing was broken. And Mr. Schwartz was going to make him fight again and again until he was killed! She'd been so glad to escape, she hadn't tried to get him back. For a few wonderful minutes she'd had him, and in another second or two, she'd lost him again. Tears stung her cheeks. Amanda slowed down to a walk and wiped her face with the back of her hand. But if Daddy went to see Mrs. Schwartz — and he just had to — she'd get another chance. With Daddy there, it would be safe. He wouldn't let Mr. Schwartz hurt her. Hurry! she told herself. Hurry! Mrs. Schwartz was waiting, and so was Mazda! She started to run again.

She ran on and on. When she slowed down to catch her breath, she noticed that the sky was changing color. A cloud bank rose up from the north and swept across the low-lying sun, hanging a veil of greenish light over the earth. A spear of lightning pierced the gloom, and thunder rumbled in the distance. A storm! Thank goodness she was now only a few sprints from the Bestwicks'. When she ran up the driveway, not a leaf stirred. The barking of the Bestwicks' dogs echoed in the hot, still air. The sound came closer. She could see the black dog running toward her, with the spotted one not far behind. They were out! Someone had let them out! When she rounded the curve, she stopped and stared. A wave of fear swept over her. Daddy's car was gone!

❧ *Chapter 12* ❧

*A*manda pounded on the Bestwicks' door. The cool wind was stirring up dust now and whipping the trees. When she looked up, silver leaves seemed to churn against the black sky. A tin can spun across the yard, and a tumbleweed blew up on the porch. The dogs whimpered and crawled under the steps. She pounded again. Wasn't anybody home? And where could Daddy have gone? Why did he leave her? To teach her a lesson? Maybe he had a call to go somewhere else. He'd surely be back. Surely! Or would he? Maybe he was mad at her and didn't want her anymore. No question about it, she'd been bad lately. Letting him think she'd come along just to be with him. And running away when she should have stayed. And sneaking off to a bootlegger's farm, and nearly getting kidnaped. Daddy had every right to leave her. And that wasn't all. She felt worse all the time about snooping into Daddy's records. And another thing. She hated Margaret sometimes. Her own sister! She was being punished. She was sure of it.

She pounded harder. The wind howled so she couldn't tell if anyone was in the house. Even if they were yelling "come in" at the top of their lungs, she wouldn't be able to hear them. While she stood there, it had grown dark as night. Lightning flashed, and thunder roared. Big rain drops pelted the porch roof, then spilled down in waves. No one came. She'd feel a lot safer inside. She tried the door. It opened.

The front room was dark. Where was everyone? What about the sick person Daddy had come to see? In a back bedroom, probably. She closed the door and watched the storm from the window. It wasn't as loud and scary in here. She wondered if going into somebody's house without asking made her a burglar. Then, behind her, she heard footsteps. She turned around. Framed in a doorway, stood a man in overalls carrying a lit kerosene lamp. His clothes looked wet. She hoped he wasn't mean like Mr. Schwartz.

"Your name happen to be Albee?" he asked.

"Yes," said Amanda. "Where's my Daddy?"

"He should be along in a few more minutes. We was all goin' plumb crazy tryin' to figger out what happened to ya. So he took a spin around in the car to look. He'll be back if he don't get stuck in the mud."

Amanda took a deep breath and smiled. He sounded all right. Must be Mr. Bestwick. And Daddy was coming for her! He still wanted her! She wished he'd hurry. Mrs. Schwartz needed him badly!

"Sorry to come in without asking," she said. "I knocked but nobody answered." She felt so thirsty she could hardly talk.

"I woulda' let ya in, but I had to go out and see to the cows."

"Could I have a drink of water, please?" she asked.

"You sure can, young lady. You jes' stay right here by the window and keep an eye out fer yer daddy, and I'll bring it to you."

Amanda watched the sky grow lighter and the rain fill hollows in the yard to form pools of all sizes. When Daddy came back, she'd have a problem, and she had to decide what to do about it. If she told him everything — about almost being kidnaped — he might not take her along to see Mrs. Schwartz. And what's worse, he would probably refuse to go. No. She couldn't tell him about this afternoon until it was all over, Mrs. Schwartz's life saved, and Mazda back home where he belonged. Back home? She'd hide him again, but in a better place. She'd find one.

"Here you are, young lady." Mr. Bestwick came out of the kitchen carrying a tin cup. Amanda ran up to him and stood in the middle of the room gulping the cool water. Mr. Bestwick took her place by the window.

"Here he is," he said, "comin' up the drive. Glad he didn't get stuck." He opened the front door. Amanda heard the tires squish through the puddles.

She handed Mr. Bestwick the cup on her way out. "Thanks!" From the porch, she waved her arms as the car came to a stop. "Here I am, Daddy! Here I am!" Her shoes gurgled as she ran through driving rain. By the time she opened the car door and sank into the front seat, she was sopping wet.

Daddy stuck his head out the car window. "Much obliged to you, Frank!" Mr. Bestwick nodded and went back in the house.

"What happened, Kitten?" Daddy asked, as he

turned the car around. "I came out of the house and found a carful of dogs and no Amanda."

"I didn't want them to follow me." Amanda had no time to lose. "Oh, Daddy!" she cried. "Mrs. Schwartz who lives down the road is terribly sick and asked me to call a doctor for her. She didn't know who I was, so I told her and said you were at the Bestwicks' and that I'd tell you to come. She said she'd be waiting for you, Daddy."

Daddy stopped the car, but the motor was still running. "Slow down, Little Kitten. What in the world were you doing at the Schwartzes'?"

"I started walking and pretty soon I was at the Schwartzes'." It was all true, thought Amanda, but it felt like a lie.

"Started walking?"

"Oh, Daddy! She came to the window . . . Her face was all white."

"Who? What window?"

"Her bedroom window. Mrs. Schwartz! And she looked just terrible. She said her side hurt." Amanda patted her side. "Right here."

"Right there, huh?" Daddy's brows came together.

"She said it felt like a knife."

"A knife, huh? Bad sign. Why didn't she call me herself?"

"They don't have a telephone, Daddy. So she sent me."

"Well, I suppose it wouldn't hurt to drive over there. If she wants me to come."

"Oh, she does, Daddy! She said she'd be waiting."

135

"Which way is it, Amanda?"

Amanda pointed. "That way."

Rain lashed against the car, and the roadbed had softened into a river of brown mud. Daddy jerked the steering wheel from side to side to keep the car from sliding into the ditch.

"That's the place, Daddy! Right up there."

When they turned into Schwartzes' driveway, it was growing dark again. Night was coming on. As Daddy pulled up to the house, Mr. Schwartz hurried through the rain to the car as if he'd expected them. Amanda wondered why. Maybe he'd been waiting for someone else. Or maybe his wife told him she'd sent for the doctor. When Daddy lowered the window, spray from the downpour spat at Amanda's cheek. She was hoping Mr. Schwartz wouldn't mention anything about this afternoon.

"What're you doin' here, Doc?" Mr. Schwartz shouted. Amanda wondered if he thought Daddy came to bawl him out for mistreating her.

"Lester, I hear your wife's sick and wants me to see her," said Daddy. Amanda was glad Daddy'd left her out of it.

"She ain't got any right to send for doctors," said Mr. Schwartz. "If any doctors are called around here, I'm the one who does it. Go on home, Doc. We don't need you."

"How is Mrs. Schwartz feeling?" asked Daddy.

"She's been bellyachin' off and on since way last fall. If you ask me, she's just lazy."

Just lazy! thought Amanda. Had he looked at her lately?

Daddy stared at the steering wheel. "Is she in bed?"

"Yep," said Mr. Schwartz. "She and the bed have taken a real likin' to one another."

Then Daddy spoke in his gentlest voice. "Lester, I appreciate your trying to spare me the trouble of calling on your wife, but since I'm here, I'll just go on in and check her over."

Mr. Schwartz stood in front of the car door so that Daddy couldn't get out. "What's it goin' to cost me?"

"Well, if there's nothing wrong with Mrs. Schwartz, there won't be any charge at all. Amanda and I were in the neighborhood anyway."

Amanda noticed that Mr. Schwartz didn't even glance at her. It was a relief. As soon as Daddy went in, she'd look for Mazda.

"What if something's wrong with her?" asked Mr. Schwartz. "What'll it cost me then?"

"That depends on what I have to do." As Daddy lifted the door handle, a flash of lightning startled Mr. Schwartz so that he jumped away from the car.

Daddy grabbed his doctor case and got out. "Come in, Amanda. It's pretty nasty out here."

"I'll come in a little while," she said.

Thunder crashed, and Daddy followed Mr. Schwartz into the house. Amanda wasn't crazy about looking for Mazda in a rainstorm, but she was sure it would be her last chance. First, she'd try the chicken coop where she looked this afternoon. She slipped out of the car. Rain pelted her face and head and took her breath away. Heading toward the back yard, she stepped through mud and sloshed through puddles and wet weeds. Behind the house, a lightning flash outlined the coop. Thunder roared. Soaked to the skin and shivering, she looked in. She smelled the sour odor of damp feathers and heard the clucking of chickens, but she couldn't see anything. When lighning flickered, Amanda saw only hens. No Mazda. Amanda wondered if she'd ever see him again. Just to be sure, she waited for another flash and saw one rooster in a far corner, but he was all white. She ran around to the far side of the house where she'd first seen him this afternoon. From the window, a glow of light streaked across the wet tire. This time, no gunnysack rested in its center. Glancing through the window, Amanda saw Daddy bending over Mrs. Schwartz's bed. Mr. Schwartz stood behind him, holding up a kerosene lamp. Amanda felt pleased that she'd brought Daddy here to help Mrs. Schwartz. But Mazda! She had to find him! There was another place. She'd try it.

With the help of lightning flashes, Amanda found her way back to the fence, where she last saw Mazda near the feet of the man named Joe. She ran her fingers through tall wet grass. No Mazda. The trees above whispered *shhhhh* in the wind. Her teeth chattered from the cold. She couldn't stay out here much longer.

Her tears mingled with the rain as she ran toward the house. Where had they hidden him? Maybe he was dead. A pair of eyes glowed from under the porch. A cat, probably. The porch! Hadn't Jack once hidden

Mazda under Mrs. Schooler's porch? She'd look. She crouched down and peered into the blackness under the steps. Nothing but cat eyes. Then, with a burst of light from the sky, she spotted a gunnysack behind a cement post. She reached for it and slid it out. When she lifted it up, it moved in her arms. She felt feet and feathers. It was Mazda!

"Buck, buck, buck!" he said.

"Oh, Mazda!" whispered Amanda. She held him close. "We'll leave you in the sack for now, but you're going home with me!" Trembling with fear and joy, she ran with him and put him on the floor of the car in back. She hoped he wouldn't make any noise. If Mr. Schwartz caught her a second time, no telling what would happen. She spoke to Mazda in hushed tones. "I'm going in the house now to get warm, but I'll be back."

❦ *Chapter 13* ❦

*A*manda stood inside the back door and watched the storm. Her wet clothes clung to her skin and dripped on the floor. She shivered as she listened to the voices from the bedroom.

"Ooooooooh, am I going to die, Doctor?"

Daddy's tone was soothing. "Not if we can help it, Mrs. Schwartz."

Lightning flickered, and Amanda caught a glimpse of the kitchen. The pattern on the linoleum rug was nearly gone except for patches here and there, like islands on a strange map. In the far shadows stood the cookstove. In Amanda's home, the cookstove meant warmth and food and laughter, but here it became a lurking black monster — cold, silent, and terrifying. When thunder rolled, so that she couldn't hear any more talk, she worried that Mr. Schwartz might find Mazda in their car. She should have put those other gunnysacks on top of him. And where was Jack? she wondered. He didn't seem to be here.

Holding the kerosene lamp, Mr. Schwartz followed Daddy out of the bedroom. They stood in a circle of pale light.

Mr. Schwartz's eyes glittered with rage. "She had no business callin' you, Doc."

Daddy's face looked grave. "It's appendicitis. She has the chronic type that flares up and calms down and flares again. Sometimes it goes on like that for years until it bursts. Then it's a killer. This attack is very serious, Lester. It could be her last."

"What are you tryin' to tell me, Doc?" Mr. Schwartz's eyes narrowed.

"With the storm and the bad roads, she's at least an hour from the hospital. The delay would be dangerous."

"And just what do you intend to do about it?" Mr. Schwartz spat the words between clenched teeth.

"I'll have to operate immediately."

Amanda shuddered. An operation! They'd be here a long time! With Mazda in the car!

Mr. Schwartz stepped closer to Daddy. "Did I hear you say 'operate'? Here? In this house?"

"Yes."

Mr. Schwartz stomped his foot and shouted, "Over my dead body!"

Daddy spoke quietly. "I've performed surgery in kitchens many times, Lester. The only ones I've lost are those who waited too long. We haven't a minute to lose."

Surgery in kitchens! thought Amanda. She'd have to get out of here fast. Guts made her sick. But something about the way Mr. Schwartz looked into Daddy's face held her frozen to the spot.

"You never miss a chance to cut somebody up, do ya, Doc?" he said. "I'm about paid up now, so you're tryin' to keep the money rollin' in. Nice racket you got there. And with all them big words ya throw around, you could be lyin' and nobody'd know it."

Amanda felt goose bumps as she hugged her arms. How dare he talk to Daddy like that?

"Look, Lester," said Daddy, "I'm not doing this for pleasure or money. I've already had an exhausting day. I'd rather be at home right now having supper with my family."

Amanda watched as Mr. Schwartz put the lamp down on a washstand, and walked over to a dark corner of the kitchen. When he came back into the light, she gasped. He was holding a shotgun! He didn't point it at Daddy. He held it down at his side. Amanda shook uncontrollably. Mr. Schwartz might shoot them both. That man named Joe wasn't here to talk him out of it. And neither was Jack. It was all her fault. She'd asked Daddy to come. But if she hadn't — Mrs. Schwartz! It was terrible.

Daddy spoke in a calm voice. "You won't be needing that gun, Lester, but I will need your help. We'll have to move your wife to the kitchen table and we'll need some boiling water for my instruments."

Mr. Schwartz took a step backward. "What if I say no, Doc?"

"Then your wife will die."

Mr. Schwartz put the barrel of the gun on the floor and leaned on it like a cane. "Maybe it's her time to go. How do you know it ain't the Lord's will?"

Daddy sighed. "All I know, Lester, is that it's my duty to save her if I can."

"If I shot you, you wouldn't be able to operate, would you, Doc?"

Amanda stood in the shadows, frozen with terror, scarcely able to breathe.

"Don't be a fool, Lester Schwartz." Daddy sounded angry, and his eyes turned dark and fiery. "A lot of people know I'm in the neighborhood. This would be one of the first places they'd look, and tomorrow you'd be in prison. Another thing, Lester. Your wife is critically ill. If you refuse to let me treat her, and she dies, I could charge you with a crime."

Mr. Schwartz lowered his head and peered up at Daddy. "Yeah. I can see it now. Your four-bit words against my nickel ones."

"That's right, Lester. Put that gun away and help me."

Mr. Schwartz stared at Daddy in silence for several seconds. "You highfalutin doctors and lawyers think you have the whole world sewed up in the palm o' yer hand, dontcha? And all you have to do is give it a squeeze to get whatcha want. I'll help ya, Doc, but only because ya boxed me in. But you git one thing straight. If she dies because of your butcherin', I'll finish you off. Somebody oughta put an end to this con game you're runnin', and it might as well be me." Mr. Schwartz set the gun on the washstand and followed Daddy to the kitchen table.

That gun! thought Amanda. It had to go! She couldn't allow Mr. Schwartz to be in the same room with a gun. She'd stay as quiet as possible, then pounce on it the first chance she got.

Daddy looked at the table. "It's a little small."

Mr. Schwartz flipped a latch underneath and pulled the two halves apart.

"Now, Lester," said Daddy, "we'll have to take off that closet door over there and cover it with a clean sheet." In a minute, Mr. Schwartz unhinged the door, and he and Daddy took it into the bedroom.

They were gone. For a minute? Maybe two? Amanda couldn't just stand there shaking. She had to do something. Even with Daddy here, she felt terribly alone. It seemed like he'd forgotten about her. He was too busy trying to save Mrs. Schwartz to think about anything else — even the danger to himself. On tiptoe, Amanda crept up to the washstand. Mr. Schwartz must never pick that gun up again. Never! But as Amanda's icy hands reached out to grab it, she heard groans and shuffling feet. They were coming! It was too late! She darted away from the washstand. Mr. Schwartz was backing through the doorway and holding up one end of the sheet-draped door. On it lay Mrs. Schwartz. Daddy held the other end, and they carried her into the kitchen. Then they laid her crosswise over the gap in the table. Mrs. Schwartz was a fat woman. Covered with a sheet, she made a snowy hill in the middle of the kitchen.

"Where are you taking me?" she moaned.

Daddy spoke to her in a soothing voice. "To the kitchen, Mrs. Schwartz. You have an inflamed appendix. We'll put you to sleep and remove it. You should feel better in a few days."

"Oh, Doctor!" said Mrs. Schwartz. "I'm so glad you came."

Listening to Mrs. Schwartz, Amanda was almost glad they came, too. But the gun!

"Is there a fire in the cookstove, Lester?" asked Daddy.

"I'll have one goin' in a few minutes."

The thought of being in the same room not only with an armed Mr. Schwartz, but with an operation, filled Amanda with panic. Yet she couldn't run to the car now. She had to wait for a chance to hide the gun.

"Amanda, come here," said Daddy. He put his hands on her shoulders and drew her close. "We'll have to work together to save this woman's life. Promise me you'll listen carefully and do whatever I ask, and do it quickly."

An invisible belt tightened around Amanda's chest, so that she couldn't breathe. Help with an operation? This was bad trouble, and she was just a kid, the little kid everybody sent to the store, because she couldn't do any of the grown-up things. She'd go to the store now, right this minute, if she could. She always high-tailed it out of the kitchen whenever Mama cleaned chickens. An operation would be a hundred times worse. Mrs. Schwartz was at least a hundred times as big as a chicken. There'd be guts all over the place. What if she fainted? Daddy's eyes searched her face. He needed her. She could tell.

"I promise, Daddy."

He patted her on the back. "Good girl. Now get some water from the pump in the back yard and take it over to the stove."

Amanda breathed easier knowing that her first chore would take her farther away from Mrs. Schwartz's insides. But at the same time, she'd be leaving Mr. Schwartz and his gun alone with Daddy. She'd hurry. As she opened the back door, she eyed the washstand. She couldn't grab the gun now, because Mr. Schwartz kept turning around every which way as he built the fire.

Later, after Daddy had washed Mrs. Schwartz's stomach, Amanda, Daddy, and Mr. Schwartz scrubbed with homemade brown soap. Amanda's hands itched.

"Germs hate lye soap," Daddy said.

Amanda sat on a box by the stove waiting for Daddy to tell her what to do next. The fumes from the ether he was using to put Mrs. Schwartz to sleep made her feel dizzy. She walked to the open door for a breath of fresh air. Rain still spattered on the steps and streamed off the porch roof.

While Mr. Schwartz held up the lamp, Daddy took Mrs. Schwartz's pulse. "She's asleep now." Daddy slipped on a pair of rubber gloves. "We can proceed. Lester, please bring that lamp down this way a bit."

Amanda studied Mr. Schwartz's face. His bushy brows were drawn together. He looked meaner than ever, though he did everything Daddy asked. The gun still lay across the washstand, an instant away from his reach. Daddy was working in his shirt sleeves. His suit coat lay on the washstand, partly covering the gun.

As the minutes ticked by, the quiet was broken by Mrs. Schwartz's heavy breathing and the clanking of Daddy's instruments as he picked them up and put them down in a dishpan. Amanda's breath came easier. Maybe Daddy wouldn't need her anymore. But how could she get that gun without being seen? She gazed out into the rain-soaked back yard and closed her eyes. She'd gotten Daddy into this mess. It was all her fault. Tears slipped down her cheeks. Maybe it was a nightmare, and she'd wake up safe and sound in her bed in Prairie Bend.

Suddenly Amanda heard a different sound, a dull thud. The floor shook, and everything got darker. Then she heard the tinkle of broken glass. Squinting in the twilight, Amanda saw Daddy still bending over Mrs. Schwartz, but she couldn't see Mr. Schwartz at all.

"Amanda, come here," said Daddy.

When Amanda ran around the table, she saw Mr. Schwartz lying on the floor with his eyes closed. The oil lamp chimney lay in several pieces on the floor. Mr. Schwartz still held onto the base, but the flame had gone out.

Without looking up, Daddy said, "Mr. Schwartz fainted. You and I will have to finish this job ourselves. Bring me my flashlight. It's in the car trunk. The key's in my coat pocket on the washstand. I'll hold steady here until you're back."

With key in hand, Amanda paused a second. Daddy was too busy to watch her, and Mr. Schwartz, sprawled on the floor, looked harmless enough. Being careful not to touch the trigger, Amanda lifted the gun and ran with it to the car. If Daddy noticed what she did, he gave no sign.

The shotgun lay across the car bumper as Amanda struggled with the key. What if she couldn't unlock the trunk? What if Mr. Schwartz woke up and found her with his gun? Would she have the nerve to point it at him? She'd have to, she decided. She looked over her shoulder, but the house was still dark and quiet. What if he had another gun? A pistol? Or a machine gun like they have in gangster movies? Her fingers, cold and wet with rain, trembled as she twisted the key this way and that. Finally the trunk opened, and she placed the gun inside. Then she grabbed the flashlight and locked the trunk. She splashed through puddles as she ran into the house. Mr. Schwartz was still lying on the floor, unconscious.

"Does it work?" asked Daddy.

Amanda pushed the button with her thumb and circles of light flashed across the room.

"Stand over here and hold the light steady," said Daddy, "right on the incision. That's a good girl. Look the other way and take deep breaths if you start to feel sick."

At first, Amanda looked at the floor and then at the ceiling. Now and then, she stole a glimpse of the operation to see if she could stand it. It wasn't as bloody and messy as she'd expected. Not nearly as gory as watching Mama clean a chicken. She took several deep breaths, though. She couldn't faint. She wouldn't. It would be rotten of her to leave Daddy when he needed her. Gradually, Amanda became interested in the way Daddy tied off the appendix and snipped it out. Daddy explained the operation as he went along.

Nearly finished, Daddy was stitching up the skin on Mrs. Schwartz's side, when Amanda heard a shuffling sound and Mr. Schwartz's voice.

"Somebody hit me and broke my lamp."

It was all Amanda could do to hold the light steady. He'd soon notice his gun was gone.

"You fainted, Lester." Daddy didn't look up. He kept right on sewing.

"Faintin's for women," said Mr. Schwartz. "Somethin' hit me."

"Something hit you, all right," said Daddy. "It was the floor."

Scared as she was, Amanda smiled a little.

"I don't need no smart-mouthed horse doctor tellin' me I fainted."

"Lester, it's no disgrace to faint," said Daddy. "I fainted the first time I watched an operation."

Mr. Schwartz's feet crunched over the broken lamp pieces as he walked to the washstand. "Where's my gun?" he shouted. "Somebody stole my gun! Gimme back my gun, Doc!"

Amanda's stomach felt as if she'd swallowed a brick, and her heart throbbed in her ears. She was afraid she was going to be sick.

Daddy wiped off his instruments and put them into his doctor case. "Lester Schwartz! I have been standing right here in this spot for a half hour, too busy to think about anything but your wife's operation. Incidentally, the surgery went well. We caught the appendix in time. In a few minutes it would have burst."

Mr. Schwartz whirled around and pointed to Amanda. "That little sneak thief took my gun!"

Sneak thief! Amanda felt dizzy, a lot dizzier than when she'd looked at Mrs. Schwartz's insides. Would he tell Daddy about this afternoon? Mr. Schwartz reached for Amanda, but Daddy stood in front of her. He took the flashlight out of her hand and shined it in Mr. Schwartz's face.

"Don't touch my daughter. Lester Schwartz, you're behaving like a damn fool. Pull yourself together and help me put your wife back to bed."

Mr. Schwartz turned away from the light and mopped his brow with a blue bandanna handkerchief. Then he and Daddy walked over to the table, lifted the door with the sleeping Mrs. Schwartz on it, and carried her into the bedroom. Now that the operation was over, Amanda wanted to run out and throw more gunnysacks over Mazda. Suppose Mr. Schwartz saw him? But Daddy needed her here. She couldn't leave him alone with Mr. Schwartz. He might have another gun.

When they came back to the kitchen, Daddy spoke to Mr. Schwartz in a stern voice. "Lester, you'll have to take care of your wife when she wakes up, and she's going to be mighty sick for awhile. You're to give her only liquids for the first few days, then soft foods for the next three. Bring her in to my office on Friday. Do you think you can remember all that?" Daddy picked up his bag.

Mr. Schwartz nodded, wiped his brow with his handkerchief again, and sank into a chair. Good! thought Amanda. He seemed too weak to follow them outside.

After Amanda and Daddy got in the car, Amanda peeked in back to check on Mazda. The gunnysack wasn't moving. Good! He's asleep, thought Amanda. Daddy was just putting the key in the ignition, when Mr. Schwartz ran down the porch steps shaking his fist.

"You stole my gun! You stole my gun!"

Daddy pushed the gas pedal down hard. The engine zoomed, and the car swerved from side to side over the slippery driveway, and on past the Schwartzes' mailbox. Amanda heaved an enormous sigh as the car moved steadily along the wet country road toward Prairie Bend. Amanda hoped Mazda didn't wake up. She'd hate having to explain about all that just now. If she was lucky, she might not have to explain it at all. If Mazda stayed quiet, she'd hide him when they got home, and that would be the end of it.

"That was some experience, wasn't it, Little Kitten?"

Amanda nodded. "Do you want to know where I hid the gun, Daddy?"

Daddy smiled. "I thought you'd tell me sooner or later."

"It's in the trunk." Amanda shuddered at the thought of Mr. Schwartz's gun being right there in the car with them, following them all the way into Prairie Bend.

Daddy grinned. "You're a brave young lady, Amanda. I'm proud of you. All on your own, you did what you could to save our lives. Not only that, you helped me with Mrs. Schwartz's operation. I couldn't have done it without you." He took one hand off the steering wheel and patted her knee. "Yes, Amanda. I'm proud of you."

Amanda felt a happy glow rush through her. Daddy was proud! And she hadn't even played the violin or fixed a radio. But if he found out about Mazda, he might take it all back. She got up on her knees, and pretending to look out the rear window, stole a glimpse of the gunnysack lying on the floor. It still wasn't moving. What if Mazda was dead? Maybe he hadn't had any food or water for days. And his wing didn't look right. Could he die of a broken wing? It was night, though. He was probably just sleeping. But Amanda's worries grew as the car slipped and slid on the muddy road to Prairie Bend. By the time they drove into town, Mazda still hadn't made a sound.

Amanda and Daddy didn't go straight home. They stopped at the sheriff's office where Daddy told Sheriff Spear everything Mr. Schwartz said and did while they were there. Since Amanda didn't want to bring up Mazda, she kept quiet about Mr. Schwartz's threat to lock her up in his storm cellar.

Sheriff Spear checked the chamber of Mr. Schwartz's gun. "You say he didn't point it at you?"

"No, he didn't," said Daddy.

"Well, Doc, Lester Schwartz is as mean as they come, but he's a clever old codger. He always manages to skirt the law." A hint of a smile tugged at Sheriff Spear's straight mouth as he put the gun down on his desk. "The gun isn't loaded."

Daddy and Amanda stared at each other, with open mouths.

"Anyway," said Sheriff Spear, "I'll be glad to drive out in the morning and give him a good tongue-lashing."

As they were leaving, Daddy turned at the door. "While you're there, Sheriff, I'd be obliged if you'd look in on Mrs. Schwartz and then give me a call when you get back."

"Be glad to, Doc," he said.

When they got in the car, Amanda glanced at the sack. Mazda wasn't moving. In a way, it was good. But how terrible it would be if he were dead!

Daddy started the engine. "I need to stop by the hospital on the way home. If there aren't any emergencies, it shouldn't take more than a few minutes. You don't mind, do you, Little Kitten?"

"Aw, Daddy!" She wanted to go home and hide Mazda, and take him out of his bag and feed him. He couldn't be dead! But what if he was?

❦ *Chapter 14* ❦

*D*addy parked the car in front of the hospital. "You'd better come in, Amanda. I don't know how long I'll be here."

When they walked in the door, one of the sisters glided toward them with an anxious look on her face.

"Oh, Doctor! We've been trying to reach you. A confinement came in about an hour ago."

Amanda knew what "confinement" meant. Some woman was having a baby. She wondered if it was Virginia Thornhill. She'd never know, because she wouldn't dare ask.

Daddy looked down at Amanda. "Sorry, Little Kitten. You must be tired. Sister Francis, this is my daughter Amanda. Can you find a comfortable spot for her? She might like to lie down a bit. And I'd appreciate it if you'd call my wife and tell her we're here."

"Certainly, Doctor."

Daddy hurried down the hall, while Amanda followed Sister Francis through a frosted glass door just off the main waiting room.

The nun smiled and pointed to a long leather couch. "Just make yourself comfortable, my dear."

"Thanks," said Amanda, but her thoughts raced.

What about Mazda? She had to know whether he was dead or alive.

"Sister," said Amanda, "I left something in the car. I'd like to go out there a minute. May I?" It was all true, but she felt like she was lying.

"Certainly," said the sister. "And when you get back, there'll be a pillow and maybe a cookie or two waiting for you."

"Gee, thanks," said Amanda. A cookie! She was starving.

Outside, it was still raining, but not so hard. When Amanda opened the rear car door, she said to herself, "Please! Please! Let him be alive!" When she lifted the bag, Mazda moved.

"BWAWK! BWAWK!" he cried.

"Oh, Mazda! Mazda! You're alive!" She held the gunnysack up to her cheek. How rough and damp it felt! How uncomfortable he must be! Amanda slid onto the back seat, closed the car door, and untied the bag. Poor thing. She just had to free him, if only for a minute, and look at his injured wing. When Amanda lifted him out, Mazda pulled himself up to his full height and stretched his good wing. The other one drooped like a half-opened fan. He shook his head until his comb wobbled. She patted him and held him close. "I'll find a new place for you, Mazda, but right now, I'm going to put you in a dry gunnysack. You won't have to stay in it very long." She reached for one of the bags lying on the seat.

"Buck, buck, buck, buck BUH KAWP!"

Amanda knew it. Mazda was trying to tell her something. She hesitated, holding the sack in one hand and Mazda's legs in the other.

"BWAWK! BWAWK! BWAWK!" cried Mazda.

Amanda sighed and put the sack down on the seat. "I don't blame you, Mazda. After what you've been through, I wouldn't want to go back in a sack either. Tell you what. I'll let you out, so you can walk around in the car for a while. Then I'll come back here and tie you up before Daddy gets through. How does that sound?"

"Buck, buck, buck, buck."

"Better, huh? All right, then." Amanda slipped out the car door and shut it carefully, as Mazda stood looking up at her from the back seat. She waved at him through the window. "Bye, Mazda. See you soon."

In the hospital waiting room, Amanda opened the frosted glass door. She saw a pillow and a folded sheet lying on the couch. Nearby, on a table, stood a glass of milk and a plate with two cookies on it. She drank the milk and ate one of the cookies. She stashed the other one away for Mazda in her damp dress pocket.

Sister Francis poked her head in the door. She carried something white over her arm. It looked like a hospital gown.

"Ah!" she said. "I see you've finished your cookies and milk."

"Thanks," said Amanda.

"I noticed you were soaked to the skin," said Sister Francis, "so I brought you a gown. I'll take your wet things down to the laundry. Sister Vincent can press them dry for you."

Part with her clothes? She couldn't run outside half naked to put Mazda in a sack. Suppose someone saw her? "Aw, that's all right," she said. "I'm not cold."

"I insist," said Sister Francis. "If you stay in those clothes, you'll surely catch pneumonia." Sister Francis smiled and stooped to untie Amanda's shoes. "Off with your dress, now."

"If you take my dress," said Amanda, "I won't be ready to go when Daddy comes."

"I wouldn't worry about that," said Sister Francis. "He's doing a first confinement. They always take longer."

A first confinement! Virginia's would be a first. "When will you bring my clothes back?" she asked.

"Before your daddy's through."

Amanda just stood there refusing to undress. Bad enough that Sister Francis had her shoes.

"I don't want to take off my clothes," said Amanda.

Sister Francis smiled. "I understand. I'll just wait outside the door while you change. Here's the gown."

There seemed to be no possible way to outsmart Sister Francis. Her gray shadow waited on the other side of the frosted glass door. Amanda hid Mazda's cookie under the pillow and changed into the gown.

At the door, Sister Francis took the wet clothes Amanda handed her. "Thank you, my dear." Then she came in, spread the sheet on the couch, and fluffed up the pillow. Amanda was afraid she might see Mazda's cookie under there, but she didn't. "It must be past your bedtime," said the Sister. "How about a little nap?"

"Isn't Daddy going to be through pretty soon?"

"I really couldn't say. Why don't you just lie down. He'll come and wake you up when he's ready to go." The nun patted the pillow.

Amanda wouldn't dare go to sleep. Just to please the sister, she'd lie down, and when she left the room, she'd get up again and wait for her clothes. Amanda stretched out on the couch.

"That's a good girl," said Sister Francis. "If I leave this door open, it'll be cooler for you." Then she turned out the light. Amanda listened to her skirts rustle down the hall until the sound faded. A glow from a distant light shimmered across the frosted glass of the open door. Amanda thought how good it was to lie down. Strange how tired she felt. It was hard to move. But she couldn't lie here. She had to get up and wait for her clothes. She'd rest another minute. She listened to crickets chirping outside an open window. Then sleep crept up on her and wrapped her in a dreamless fog.

❦ *Chapter 15* ❦

*W*hen Amanda woke up, a soft gray light filled the room. From the open window, birds sang instead of crickets. In the distance, a rooster crowed. A rooster! Mazda? Oh, no! Morning! She'd slept through the night! Was Daddy still busy? He must be! She had to run out to the car this minute and put Mazda back in his bag. When she leaped off the couch, she saw her clothes neatly folded over the back of a chair. She had just scrambled into her underwear and was pulling on her socks, when she heard Daddy's voice in the next room. He was through! She had to beat him to the car!

"She's fine, Walter," said Daddy. "She came through it very well."

Walter! Wasn't that Mr. Thornhill's first name? Amanda slipped her foot into her sock and folded it down as she listened.

"Was it a boy or a girl, Doc?"

Amanda picked up her dress and froze. Mr. Thornhill's voice.

"It'll be better for everyone if you don't know, Walter," said Daddy.

Mr. Thornhill sounded angry. "Dammit, Doc! It's my grandchild!"

Daddy spoke softly. "It's not anymore, Walter. You and Virginia signed it over to the sisters. It's theirs now. They'll take good care of it for a month or so until they can place it with a family."

Virginia had had her baby! Somehow listening to this private talk seemed worse than peeking at Daddy's records. Yet it wasn't her fault. She just happened to be here. That promise to Lucille and the eraser made her feel strangely guilty about Virginia's baby. As Amanda pulled her dress over her head, she was wondering how she could get out to the car without being seen. Impossible. She would have to walk around or between Daddy and Mr. Thornhill. Then they'd know she'd heard. Daddy might mention it, and she'd have to be especially careful to stay quiet about the records.

She tiptoed to the window and looked down. Too high to crawl out. Only one thing to do. Pretend to be asleep. And Mazda? When Mr. Thornhill left, she'd just have to dash out to the car before Daddy got there. She crept back to the couch, pulled the sheet up, and closed her eyes. Then she heard something that crushed her with sadness. Mr. Thornhill, who was always laughing and had a joke for everyone, was sobbing. The low-pitched gasps and groans were more than Amanda could bear. She turned her face to the sofa back and bit her lips. Her throat tightened and her eyes stung, but she didn't dare let herself cry. She was asleep, remember? She had to keep on pretending forever and ever. It was scary.

"How is Mrs. Thornhill holding up under all this?" asked Daddy.

Mr. Thornhill's voice quavered. "She's heartbroken. We decided she'd be better off at home this morning. Doc, I just couldn't send my daughter away and have her go through this all alone. And I couldn't leave Prairie Bend. My whole life is here."

"You're a good man, Walter," said Daddy.

"Doc," said Mr. Thornhill, "I may tell some lies about this thing. I thought I'd let you know beforehand." Mr. Thornhill's voice sounded stronger.

"Walter," said Daddy, "I've never said a word about this case from the beginning, and I don't intend to start now. Good luck."

Amanda could hardly believe what she was hearing. Lies! Were they as bad as she'd always thought? As Daddy had just said, Mr. Thornhill seemed like such a good man. Maybe secrets weren't as bad as lies, but her own were growing heavier, like chains dragging behind her. What a relief it would be to shake them off and move freely again.

Amanda heard Daddy's footsteps approach. He patted her head. She sat up, stretched, and faked a yawn. She hoped it looked more natural than it felt. Daddy was smiling at her, but his eyes were moist.

"Ready to go home, Little Kitten?"

"Sure, Daddy." Her throat ached terribly from bottled up tears. She wouldn't cry! She couldn't. She needed the eraser more than ever now.

"Meet me out at the front desk," said Daddy. "I have some forms to fill out."

"I'll just meet you at the car," said Amanda.

"All right. I'll be along in a minute or two."

A minute or two! Amanda slipped on her shoes without bothering to tie them and, passing Daddy at the front desk, dashed out the hospital door. She was scampering down the steps when she heard a rooster crow. As she ran toward the car, she saw Mazda standing on the back seat, his bill wide open, head thrown back.

"Err — err — ERR — er — RUHR!"

Amanda lunged into the car and grabbed Mazda's legs. "Be quiet, Mazda. You mustn't do that. You'll get us both in trouble." As she picked up a gunnysack, she saw Daddy hurrying down the hospital steps. She tucked Mazda into the sack and looked for the piece of twine to tie it up with. She'd untied it in the dark last night. What had she done with it? It wasn't on the floor or seat. Gone! There was no time! Daddy was halfway to the car. She tucked the end of the sack under Mazda and laid him on the floor. "Don't you dare make noise or try to get out now, Mazda." Amanda crawled over the seat back and was sitting in front when Daddy opened the door.

"Well, Amanda, it'll be good to get home," said Daddy. "It's been a long night."

Thoughts tumbled about in Amanda's head with such speed she couldn't talk. Her worry that Mazda might get out of his untied sack couldn't drown out the sound of Mr. Thornhill's sobs ringing in her ears. She heard them over and over again.

"What's the matter, Little Kitten? Tired?"

"Not very," said Amanda. For the moment, Mazda was quiet. Maybe the darkness inside the sack had a calming effect. She hoped so. But she couldn't stop thinking about Virginia and Mr. Thornhill. It seemed that the secret she'd kept for so many months was pushing her into a corner, so that she couldn't behave naturally. And lies! They tugged at her and teased her. Were they wrong? Didn't Mr. Thornhill say he was going to lie? Why didn't Daddy try to stop him? If she kept thinking about Mr. Thornhill, she'd be sure to say something. But it wasn't like her to be quiet. Daddy would notice. She'd talk, but carefully. She knew how to be careful.

"Is lying bad, Daddy?"

"Yes, Amanda, generally speaking," he said. "But there are times when good people feel it might be cruel to others if they told the whole truth. I've seen people go through situations like that."

"Like Mr. Thornhill?" One second of heavy silence throbbed into five. Amanda couldn't believe she'd said that. She clapped both hands over her mouth. This spill wasn't water. It was ink, soaking through invisible secrets, staining them black for all to see.

Daddy waited several more seconds before he spoke, then, "Amanda, did you hear me talking to Mr. Thornhill this morning?"

Amanda nodded. Tears streamed down her cheeks, and sobs shook and tore at her whole body. "I promised! I promised!" she cried, "I just can't stand it anymore. I can't stand it!"

"You promised what?" Daddy pulled over to the side of the road, stopped the car, and put his arms around her. "What can't you stand?"

When the sobbing died down, she said, "One day,

when I cleaned your office, Lucille put the charts on your file cabinet so I wouldn't see them, but I peeked anyway, and saw Virginia Thornhill's. Lucille made me promise never to tell anyone. She gave me an eraser to remind me. I never said a word till now." She looked up and studied the lines in Daddy's face, but she couldn't tell what he was thinking. "Daddy, are you going to spank me and fire Lucille?"

Daddy loosened his hold on her and looked into her eyes. "It was wrong for you to look at the charts. I'm sure you understand that, don't you?"

Amanda nodded.

"It seems you've already suffered for what you did," said Daddy. "Maybe that's punishment enough. And it sounds as though Lucille did the right thing." Daddy smiled. "If you had to spill the beans, you chose a harmless way to do it." He patted Amanda on the back. "Feel better?"

Amanda nodded and wiped her nose. No spanking! No firing! At first, she couldn't believe that this terrible pressure inside her had finally burst. It was like an explosion going off in the desert, hurting no one. When the fear stopped, she felt joyous relief.

Daddy started the car. "Amanda, you may be surprised to hear this, but I know just what you were going through. Only I feel it most of the time. It's like the secrets of the world are all bottled up and churning around inside me."

Amanda reached over and kissed him on the cheek. "I feel sorry for you, Daddy. I don't know how you stand it."

"I've just gotten used to it, I guess."

After a little while, Amanda asked, "Is Virginia Thornhill a bad girl?"

"Of course not, Amanda. Who said she was?"

"Just about everybody."

"Well, Amanda, I'd say she's a fine young woman who just happened to make a mistake."

"What mistake did she make, Daddy?"

He looked down at Amanda. "Have you read that book of Mama's yet?"

"No. Mama won't let me read it until I'm older."

Daddy smiled. "Well, I'm sure she's right. Your mother always knows what's best for you children."

"Aw, gee. I'll have to wait another year and a half before I know everything."

"Well, Little Kitten, if you learn everything in a year and a half, you'll have quite a jump on the rest of humanity."

"Oh, Daddy! You know what I mean."

He laughed. "Yes. I suppose I do."

Amanda heard a thumping and rustling sound coming from the floor in back. Mazda! They had such a short way to go. He just had to stay quiet!

"Do you know something, Amanda?" said Daddy. "I'm mighty proud of you for keeping that secret about Virginia. You must have been tempted to tell what you saw many times. Your mother would be proud too if we could tell her, but we can't. We must never mention it again. Ever. For Virginia's sake. Promise me you'll try to forget it."

Amanda thought about the eraser in the cigar box

and said, "Yes, Daddy. I promise." A shared secret would be easier to keep. But she was so worried about the bouncing and thudding in back that it took several seconds for her to realize what Daddy had said. He had said, "I'm proud of you" — again! But she had no time to enjoy the compliment. It was clear now that Mazda was fighting his way out of the bag. She didn't dare look back. Then she heard his good wing whip back and forth. He couldn't do this to her! He just couldn't!

"Buck, buck," he muttered. Then, in a voice that could have carried for miles in the open country, he cried, "EHRR — ehrr — EHRR — err — RUHR!"

Amanda scooted down in the seat and covered her eyes as the car skidded to a stop. There was a pause. To Amanda, it seemed like minutes. Finally, Daddy spoke.

"Amanda, since yesterday afternoon, the car has gone from dog kennel to chicken coop. I'd say you have some explaining to do, young lady."

Amanda swallowed. One more secret spilled. In a way it was a relief, but she knew her worries weren't over. As she climbed into the back seat and put Mazda into his bag, the story of his rescue came out in jerky bits and pieces.

After he'd heard it all, Daddy said, "Well, Amanda, I'd have to give you an *A* for affection, but an *F* for foolhardiness."

Amanda held the bagged Mazda in her lap and stroked him. "May I keep him, Daddy?"

When Daddy spoke his first word, Amanda knew his answer by the gentleness of his tone.

"Amanda," he said, "you know as well as I do that it's against the law to keep him."

Her sobs came in gasps and spasms as she clutched the bag against her chest. When Daddy turned the car around, Amanda knew by the direction he took that they were headed just outside town to Hattie's place.

A few minutes later, Hattie opened the door of her neat cottage and cried out, "Why bless my soul! If it ain't my Amanda and her daddy! What are you doing out here so early on a Sunday morning?"

Her face wet with tears, Amanda held out the bag. "Take good care of him, Hattie. His name is Mazda. It's spelled *M-a-z-d-a*. He has a broken wing and needs a bandage. He likes to be held and talked to. And he likes oatmeal every morning. But when you cook his oatmeal, let it cool a little bit before you feed it to him. He doesn't like it too hot. If you're out of oatmeal, he'll eat mashed potatoes and bacon."

Hattie raised her eyebrows and kept looking at Amanda as she took the sack. When she peeked inside, she said, "Yep. That's a fine lookin' rooster." Her brows came together. "I can tell he's goin' to miss you, Amanda," she said. "Yep, honey. He's sure gonna miss you."

On the way home from Hattie's, Amanda cried quietly. She knew it wouldn't do to make a fuss. Daddy stopped the car in front of the drugstore and turned to her.

"Well, my brave young assistant, what'll it be? Chocolate or pecan crunch?" Her two favorites.

"Pecan crunch, Daddy. Thanks." She smiled through

her tears. He was trying to help. "I've never had ice cream for breakfast before."

"Neither have I," he said, "but I think it's a good idea. Will two quarts be enough for everyone?"

She wiped her eyes with the backs of her hands and nodded.

As they all sat around the table eating ice cream, Amanda noticed that Hal, Margaret, and Mama were dressed up for church. Not Grandpa; he never went. Then Daddy told the story of their visit at the Schwartzes', and how Amanda rescued Mazda.

"You both shoulda had better sense than to go out there. I coulda told you that," said Grandpa.

"I want you all to know how proud I am of Amanda," said Daddy. "Her bravery and quick thinking helped me through a difficult time. Even when she knew the situation was dangerous, she helped a woman who would have died otherwise. Yes. Amanda has courage. Real courage. The kind that counts."

When she thought about all those compliments in one day, Amanda weighed the cost in sadness and fear and decided that it was worth it, especially now that it was over, or mostly over.

"Well, I'm glad the two of you are safe," said Mama, "and I want you both to have a good sleep while we're in church. I'll wake you up for Sunday dinner."

"Sounds like heaven to me," said Daddy.

Amanda woke up several hours later to the smell of chicken frying and the clatter of the dining room table being set. She wiped away another tear for Mazda and joined the others in the kitchen. Hal was sliding the pan out from under the icebox to empty it. Margaret was taking water glasses out of a cabinet, and Mama was frying chicken over the summer cookstove with the coal oil burners. Then Daddy walked in. Barefoot and in his shirt sleeves, he looked sleepy. He put his arms around Mama and kissed her hair.

"How was church, Martha?" he asked.

Mama turned to him and said, "Howard, the strangest thing happened. Walter Thornhill stood up just after Reverend Matthews preached his sermon and said he had an announcement to make."

Hal came in the door with the empty icebox pan. "Yeah. He walked right up to the front of the congregation."

"We all thought he was going to preach another sermon," said Margaret.

"Well?" said Daddy.

Amanda knew. It would be the lie. She wondered what it was and what Daddy would say about it.

Mama sighed and turned the sizzling chicken. "He said his daughter Virginia had had an operation early this morning to remove a large tumor and asked us all to pray for her recovery. Then after church he told Tess Harpool that the tumor had weighed seven pounds." Mama turned to Daddy and searched his face with her eyes. "Howard, is that true?"

Daddy went to the kitchen table and sank into a chair. Amanda thought his eyes looked shadowy and tired. "Come here," he said, "all of you." The four of them circled around and looked at Daddy. Then he stared at each one of them as if he intended to burn a hole in each. His voice was stern.

"As far as I'm concerned," he said, "the Virginia Thornhill case is closed. Closed. No member of my family is to mention her case again. Ever. In my presence or anywhere else. Do you understand?"

"Yes, Howard," said Mama in a quiet voice. "We all understand."

Amanda knew then that she would never be able to forget the eraser.

❧ Chapter 16 ❧

*T*he hot July sun beat down on Amanda's head as she walked toward downtown Prairie Bend. She was on her way at last. To Hattie's place. Mama had finally agreed to let her walk there by herself, through downtown and across the railroad tracks. She had promised to obey a list of safety rules a mile long. She was going, not only to visit Mazda, but to show Hattie the newspaper article. Hattie had once said she didn't take the paper. Amanda had pasted the clipping on a piece of cardboard so it wouldn't wear out with all the handling. The headline said, "Doctor's Young Daughter Hides Gun and Assists Father with Surgery." It had come out three weeks ago: the story of the operation at the Schwartzes'. Mr. Schwartz's name wasn't mentioned, but everybody in town knew whose house it was. Daddy said Sheriff Spear probably leaked the story to the newspaper. Amanda's friends and Hal and Margaret often asked her to tell the story of that terrible evening. After her adventure at the Schwartzes', Amanda didn't mind being so different from Margaret and Hal. Though she knew she could never be like them, Amanda felt just as important as her brother and sister. She no longer felt like a worthless little kid.

Amanda had just walked past Thornhill's store and was crossing the street, when she heard a familiar voice behind her. On the other side, she turned around.

"Hey, kid!"

It was him. Jack. Walking toward her, carrying a big bundle of what looked like clothes in one hand and an envelope in the other. She was surprised.

"Are you moving away?" she asked.

He held up the knapsack. "Soon as the four-forty comes through. Do me a favor, kid, will you?"

Amanda couldn't imagine why she should do Jack a favor, after he had stolen Mazda. He smiled at her with his lopsided grin.

She looked straight at him, and her face stayed cool. She was proud of herself. "What do you want me to do?"

He held out the envelope. "Take this in to Ginny while I wait. She's workin' in her Dad's store."

"Why don't you give it to her yourself?"

"It's her old man. I can't go in there. He'd throw me out."

Amanda thought how strange it was. There was a time she couldn't go into Thornhill's store because of Jack. Now he couldn't go. "Why?" she asked. "Doesn't he like you?"

Jack slung the knapsack over his shoulder. "We got along great until he found out what my last name was."

His last name! Amanda had never known it, but she'd wondered about it once. "What is your last name?" she asked.

He studied her face. "Schwartz."

Amanda felt her mouth fly open. Embarrassed, she closed it and swallowed. Her heart was pounding. "You mean — ?"

"Yeah. He's my old man." He thrust the envelope toward her.

Stunned, Amanda took it. Then she looked up at him. "What's in it?"

"Why you wanta know?"

"If it's something bad, I won't do it."

He laughed under his breath. "It's OK, Miss Prim-and-Proper. It's a train ticket."

Amanda grinned. This was exciting. "To where?"

"Never mind that," he said. "I'll wait here. Just hand it to her, then come back and tell me if she took it. If she won't take it, give it back. Simple. There's a nickel in it for you."

A whole nickel! She could buy an ice cream cone! Pecan crunch!

"I'll do it."

"I'll wait."

As she crossed the street to the store, Amanda thought about Virginia. People didn't talk about her much these days. Some folks believed Mr. Thornhill's story about the tumor. Others didn't believe it, but they shut up about it out of respect for the family.

Virginia stood behind the counter, weighing nails for a customer. Amanda didn't know if it was just her imagination, but she didn't seem to smile and talk as much as she used to, though she looked as pretty as ever.

With a sober face, Virginia handed over the sack of

nails. "Thank you," she said. Her voice sounded flat. Tired. Then she looked down at Amanda. "What can I do for you, Amanda?"

"Jack told me to give you this."

Virginia stared at Amanda as she took the envelope. She opened the flap, pulled the ticket out partway, and glanced at it. Then she put it back in the envelope, ripped it in two, and tore each of the halves again. She crumpled the pieces and tossed them into the waste-basket by the cash register. One piece missed and landed on the floor near Amanda's feet.

Amanda stood there speechless. How could Virginia do such a thing? To a train ticket! And Jack was wait-ing. What should she tell him? Then Mr. Thornhill came out from the back of the store. He was carrying a pile of yellow paper.

"Well, well, well!" he said. "Look who's here! You couldn't have come at a better time. Amanda, remem-ber when you suggested I run for mayor? Well, it's all set. I'm running. And here are the handbills. I'm askin' my friends to see that every house in town gets one. I'm countin' on you and your grandpa to cover four or five blocks apiece. They're fresh off the press." He handed one to Amanda. It said, "Walter Thornhill for Mayor. A Man You Can Trust. An Honest, Reliable, Lifelong Resident of Prairie Bend."

It was the word *honest* that bothered Amanda. She bit her lower lip as she thought about Mr. Thornhill. He would be a better mayor than a lot of people she knew, and she still liked him. But was a man who had lied in church honest? She needed more time to think.

"Well, how about it, young lady? How many do you want?"

She handed the flier back to him. "I'm not going home right now, Mr. Thornhill. Maybe later."

As she turned to leave, Amanda picked up the ticket scrap by her foot. Her hand paused above the wastebasket. A train ticket was so valuable, it seemed wrong to throw away even a small corner of one. Virginia and Mr. Thornhill weren't watching. She tucked the scrap into her dress pocket and left the store.

Jack was still there. On the corner. Waiting for her. "Did you give it to her?" he asked.

"Yes."

"Did she say anything?"

"No."

"Was her old man there?"

"Yes."

He grinned. "No wonder she didn't say anything."

This was the man who stole Mazda. Because of him, Mazda had fought and gotten a broken wing. She could hurt him now if she wanted to. Pay him back. She had the scrap of ticket in her pocket. If she didn't say anything, he'd be hurt sooner or later anyhow, but maybe not as badly. Did she want to be the one to do it? She wasn't sure.

"Here, kid." He held out a nickel.

"No thanks." He wouldn't pay if he knew what had happened. She couldn't take it even when it meant pecan crunch on a cone.

"Here. Come on. That was the deal."

"No. You keep it. I have to go." She started down the street.

He followed. "You know, kid, you're all right. I heard about what you did at my old man's house."

She turned to him. "We needed you that night. You should have helped your mother when she was so sick."

Jack walked along beside her, toward the railroad tracks. "In the first place, she's not my mother."

"Not your mother? Who is she, then?"

"Schwartz's second wife. Or maybe his fourth. I don't know. He probably ran through 'em pretty fast. My ma divorced him when I was two and ran away to Chicago. Never saw him after that. I wanted to check my old man out for myself. Didn't believe my mother's stories about him. But she was right. He's one helluva mean man."

Amanda wished he wouldn't say hell, but she kept her mouth shut about it. "Where were you that night?" she asked. As they walked on, Amanda could see the railroad station with its arches and red-tiled roof.

Jack shifted his knapsack to the other shoulder. "Hitched a ride to get your daddy. By the time I got to town, he was out there already. But I didn't know it. When I got back, she'd had the operation. She's okay now."

Intent on looking both ways, Amanda said nothing as they crossed the tracks. Jack was a mixture of tough and sweet, she thought. When they reached the road on the other side, she was about to ask how he dared take Mazda off their front porch, but a train whistled.

They turned to look. The light on the engine flashed even in the daytime. It was only several blocks away. In silence, they watched it come, huffing and steaming toward them.

"Well, kid, this is where I get on."

"But that's a freight train."

"It's the way I came and it's the way I'm goin'."

Amanda fingered the ticket scrap in her pocket. She swallowed hard, but the lump in her throat wouldn't move. He bought a ticket for Virginia when he couldn't afford one for himself! The train slowed a little, but didn't stop. The cars rattled by. It was a long one.

Jack turned to her and held out his hand. Amanda pulled her hand out of her pocket, carefully leaving the ticket scrap inside. He shook it.

"So long, kid," he said. Then, with a leap that took Amanda's breath away, he hoisted himself onto a moving car and waved as he stood in an open door. She watched as he disappeared inside, and the train snaked around the bend and out of sight.

Walking on toward Hattie's house, Amanda took the scrap of ticket from her pocket. She unfolded it. The printing on it didn't make much sense, but some words were scrawled across the bottom and torn. She studied what was left of them: —— ve you. —— ways will. It wasn't hard to fill in the missing letters. Amanda swore that if anyone ever gave her a railroad ticket, she'd unfold it all the way and examine every corner of it.

❦ *Chapter 17* ❦

*A*manda pounded on Hattie's door for the third time. Why didn't she answer? She'd try the back yard. When she ran around the house, Hattie was taking clothes off the line and putting them into a basket.

"Well, saints alive! If it ain't my Amanda walkin' all the way out here by herself! Your mama phoned me you was comin'."

"Hello, Hattie." Amanda wished Hattie wouldn't talk to her as if she was a baby. She rushed over to the chicken pen. There stood Mazda surrounded by hens of many different colors. In the sunlight, Mazda's green tail feathers arched high and glowed like satin. He stood as tall and proud as ever. His injured wing seemed to have sprung back into place.

Amanda picked up Mazda and stroked his feathers. Then, carrying him in her arms, she raced over to where Hattie stood. "Hattie! His wing! It's all better."

"That took some doin', honey." Hattie folded a sheet and laid it in the basket. "Mazda and I had a real go-'round about that."

"What do you mean, Hattie?"

Hattie handed Amanda a clothespin bag. "Here.

Hold this for me. I'll tell you about it." Amanda held the clothespin bag out with her free hand.

"Well," said Hattie as she dropped a wooden pin in the bag and folded a pillowcase, "One day I came out here, and Mazda was cryin'."

"Hattie!" Amanda scoffed. "Chickens don't cry."

"That's what you think. But I know better. Big ol' rooster tears rolled down his beak so fast, he was standin' in a puddle."

Amanda giggled. Hattie was spinning one of her wild tales. It was little kid stuff, but she loved it.

Hattie continued, "Well, I was jes' plain dumbfounded. I said, 'Mazda, what you cryin' your eyes out for?' An' you know what he tol' me?"

Amanda shook her head.

"He said, 'I miss my Amanda so bad that I wanta go home right now.' Then I said, 'Mazda, you jes' shut your mouth. You're gonna live with me whether you like it or not. What's more, I'm gonna fix that wing o' yours.' Then he said, 'Fix my wing! I'm not gonna let anybody touch my wing. It hurts. Besides, whatta you know about fixin' wings?'" Hattie looked down at Amanda and shook her head. "I'll tell you, that Mazda's one sassy rooster. Then I looked him straight in the eye and said, 'Mazda, I know about a lot o' things a rooster like you never dreamed of.' Mazda, he looked up at me like he didn't believe a word of it. Then I said, 'Mazda, what's your Amanda goin' to say when she sees your wing still droopin' down and lookin' ugly?' Then he said, 'Is fixin' it gonna hurt,

Hattie?' I said, 'Sure it'll hurt, but you want it to mend right, don't you? Besides, a little pain shouldn't bother a brave fightin' rooster like you. You jes' think it over while I go inside and get my 'quipment.' Well, I went in the house and got an ol' black sock, an' a ball o' string, an' I trimmed one o' them little tongue depressors made outa wood. Then I found a roll of adhesive tape. And when I came out here, Mazda, he straightened himself up real proud and said, 'Hattie, there's only one reason I'm lettin' you do this. I want my Amanda to be proud of me.' So I tied up his legs and put the black sock over his head to keep him quiet. Then he let me line up the broken bones. I put the splint up against 'em and wrapped string around the whole thing. The tape went on over the string so it wouldn't unwind. He was real brave and didn't holler much at all. When it was over, I untied his legs and uncovered his head. When he saw his wing, he said, 'How long do I have to keep this thing on? I'd be ashamed to let Amanda see me all wrapped up like this.' I tol' him, 'You gotta leave it on till the bone grows together.' We took it off jes' before you got here.''

Amanda stroked Mazda's wing. "Thanks. I can't wait to tell Daddy what you did."

Hattie laughed. "You better not. He might have me arrested for practicin' medicine without a license."

"Where did you learn to set broken wings, Hattie?"

"Well, I seen your daddy fix Mrs. Cox's broken wrist a while back. Compared to that, Mazda's wing was an easy job."

"Mrs. Cox? Is that the ice man's wife?" asked Amanda.

"It sure is, honey. I jes' came from there an hour or so ago. I took 'em some stew and stopped in to look at their puppies."

"Puppies? Oh, Hattie! Take me there. Please?"

"Not today, honey. Some other time." Hattie folded the last piece of wash into the basket and started toward the house. Amanda, still holding Mazda, followed. At the door, she handed Hattie the clothespin bag.

"Now you put Mazda back in the pen and wait right here, honey. I got sompin' for you." Hattie went in. What could it be? Amanda wondered. Hattie made the best doughnuts in the world. Amanda put Mazda back in the pen, then sat on the back steps. She watched the leaf shadows dance on the grass and thought about Hattie's story. Mazda was lucky to be staying with someone so kind. And how good it was that she'd been able to rescue him from Mr. Schwartz — even if she couldn't keep him.

Hattie came out holding a plate with a doughnut on it — a feathery circle of golden pastry the likes of which only Hattie could make — and a tall glass of lemonade.

"Thanks, Hattie." Amanda ate part of the doughnut and gulped the cold, sweet lemonade. She hadn't realized how thirsty she'd been. Strange about Hattie, she thought. She always seemed to know what you needed before you had time to think of it yourself. Then she walked into the pen and picked up Mazda. When he had finished the rest of her doughnut, Amanda set him down. "Now you be a good rooster and mind Hattie," she said. "I'll come and see you again soon."

As they walked down the path toward the road, Amanda said, "Thanks, Hattie, for taking such good care of Mazda." Then she reached into her pocket. She'd nearly forgotten. She held out the clipping. Hattie took it and read it. When she finished, she looked down at Amanda and spoke in a quiet voice.

"You're a real hero, Amanda. You know what I'm goin' to do with this?"

Amanda hadn't intended for Hattie to keep it, but she didn't say anything.

Hattie went on. "I'm goin' to tack this up by my bed and read it every night before I go to sleep. I'm proud to know ya, honey. Proud to know ya." Hattie squeezed Amanda's shoulder. "Your ride should be comin' along here any minute."

"My ride?"

"Yep," said Hattie, "your mama and I 'ranged for you to have a ride home."

"I don't need a ride, Hattie. I can walk."

"We know that, honey, but he's acomin' anyway."

"Who? Daddy?"

"No. You'll see. Should be here in a minute."

Amanda couldn't imagine who'd be giving her a ride home. Or why. "What's this all about, Hattie?"

Hattie laughed. "Lordy, Amanda! You gonna be surprised. Me an' your daddy an' your mama, an', — I won't say who yet — got our heads together. You're gonna be downright flamgasted."

Amanda wasn't sure she wanted to be "flamgasted." Whatever that was. Feeling uneasy, Amanda swallowed.

Hattie pointed to something coming up the road. "That's it," she said. "Your ride." When it came closer and slowed down, Amanda saw that it was Mr. Cox's ice truck! It pulled up beside them and stopped.

Mr. Cox leaned out the window. "You caught me in time, Hattie. I just got home when you called."

Hattie must have called him when she went in to get the doughnut and lemonade. What was going on? Amanda wondered.

Hattie winked at Mr. Cox. "You got it with you?"

"You bet," said Mr. Cox. He got out of the truck and opened the back. Instead of ice, he pulled out a bushel basket covered with an old piece of blanket. "If you like what you see in there, Amanda, you can have it."

Amanda lifted the cloth and tossed it aside. Then, with a squeal, she reached in and lifted out a trembling bundle. "A puppy!" she shouted. It was small and white, with brown spots, floppy ears, and a tiny pink nose. "He's beautiful!" she whispered. "Is he really mine?"

"He sure is," said Mr. Cox. "Your mama and daddy agreed to it. It's all settled. I would have gotten him to you sooner, only he couldn't leave his mother. Got five more at home."

Amanda cradled the puppy in her arms. "It's the most wonderful present I ever had."

Mr. Cox tossed the empty basket into the truck. "Anybody who'll go through hellfire for a rooster deserves a fine pet."

"Hellfire's right," agreed Hattie. "Ain't no other word for what she went through."

As Mr. Cox drove her home with her new puppy, Amanda glanced out the window and saw Grandpa walking along Main Street carrying a stack of yellow paper. It looked like Mr. Thornhill's fliers.

"Would you mind giving Grandpa a ride, Mr. Cox? I want to show him my new puppy."

Mr. Cox stopped the truck. Amanda opened the door, and shouted, "Come here, Grandpa! I want to show you something!"

Grandpa set the handbills down on the seat, and fondled the puppy in his big hands. "Looks like a fine critter to me."

"Get in, Mr. Albee," said Mr. Cox. "We'll give you a lift home."

As the three of them rode home together, Grandpa pointed to the fliers. "Mr. Thornhill wants us to deliver these tomorrow. How about it, Indian Fighter?"

Amanda stroked her puppy's ears and thought hard. Mr. Thornhill had lied, but only because he'd loved his daughter so much. Hadn't she lied during these past months too? About liking Jack? And — there'd been other times . . .

"Butler's running against him," said Grandpa. "It's gonna be a tough fight."

Amanda looked up and smiled. "Sure, Grandpa. I'll help."